FAITHFUL SOLDIERS

by

R.L. Leader

First published 1989
Second softcover edition 2017
Copyright © 2017 by Targum Publishers
All rights reserved

ISBN: 9781568716411

Published by
Targum Publishers
Shlomo ben Yosef 131a/1
Jerusalem 93805
editor@targumpublishers.com

DEDICATION

To my mother, Bracha, and to the memory of my father,
Pesach—may his memory forever be a blessing.

And to my family for their encouragement, patience
and support.

PROLOGUE

IT WAS IN 1827 that Czar Nicholas I, the Iron Czar, decided to "civilize" the Jews of his realm. At first his decrees were innocuous, just a matter of adopting a family name as other Western Jews had done. No one objected. If you had money and station, you might even be given a distinguished sounding surname. But the Jews soon learned that the Czar had more sinister plans in store for them, such as forcing them to discard the *kapote* for Western dress and trim their beards.

Then, with what appeared to some as a gesture toward equality and emancipation, Nicholas opened his army's ranks to the Russian Jews. But it soon became clear that it wasn't equality that the Czar had in mind, but rather the "Russification" of the Jews: The conscripts were to serve in the army for twenty-five years, and it was assumed by the Czar and his ministers that the Jewish soldiers would return home true Russians, "positive" examples for the Jewish community to emulate. Once the details of the Czar's edict were announced, Jewish blood ran cold with terror. Non-Jews had always begun army service at the age of eighteen, but Jewish boys were to be conscripted at the age of twelve and confined in special camps for six years of preparation for army life. When the decree was implemented, it became obvious that the conditions in the camps were such that few boys would survive as Jews for even a single year.

These camps, or cantons, were run by peasant sergeants who had orders to wipe out all vestiges of "bad habits" such as refusing to eat pork or make the sign of the cross. The physical conditions were harsh and the overseers ruthless. Too frightened and too weak to withstand the fiendishness of their masters, many tender shoots were lost forever to the Jewish people.

What followed in the wake of the edict were close to three decades of horror, of widows' wails and children's shrieks, of men forced to make choices that no one could possibly make.

The Russian government gave no orderly guidelines or laws for the draft, nor did they hold individuals responsible for military service. They simply handed each community its quota, and it became the crushing burden of each community council, or *kahal*, to provide the required number of youngsters.

Faced with an impossible situation, and refusing to hand over Jewish children to the Czar's army, the Torah leadership was left with no choice but to withdraw from active participation in the *kahals*, putting all of their efforts into behind-the-scenes attempts to abolish the evil decree.

With wealthier families using legal and illegal stratagems to avoid conscription, and others simply fleeing to the forests, the *kahals* found it increasingly difficult to meet their quotas. Yet the threat of disaster for the entire community hung over its head if a *kahal* failed to provide the requisite number of conscripts. In desperation, many *kahals* were forced to resort to increasingly harsh methods of conscription, including hiring kidnappers, *khappers*, to snatch youngsters from their mothers' arms.

ONE

CLUTCHING THEIR SIDDURIM, Yaakov Yitzchak Halevi, the only son of the Kronitzer Rebbe, and his closest friend, Moshe Vohlman, the son of the Rebbe's *gabbai,* strolled home from the synagogue following evening prayers. Yankeleh, as he was affectionately called, walked with a new spring to his step, for it was just one week ago that he had been called to the Torah as a bar mitzvah. He was thinking about his new status, savoring the memory of that special day, along with the memory of still another day one month earlier, when he had stood next to his father in the synagogue and wrapped the brand new *tefillin* around his arm for the very first time. Yankeleh still found it hard to believe that he was now considered an adult and counted in the *minyan.* His father's words, recited after he had chanted his *haphtorah,* still rang in his ears: "*Baruch sheptarani meionsho shel zeh.*"

With these words his father had been freed from

religious responsibility toward him, placing it directly upon Yankeleh's own thirteen-year-old shoulders.

His pulse quickened as he remembered his father's nod of approval upon the conclusion of his meticulously prepared *drashah* and the laudatory words of Rav Lippeh Kronsberg, a leading Torah light, who had compared him to his father. "Yaakov Yitzchak's interpretation of the *sugyah* in *Pesachim* and his ability to analyze the meaning of the *Korban Pesach* with such perception speaks of an intellect beyond his years," the Rabbi had said. "We all benefited from Yaakov Yitzchak's learned *drashah*, and he has proven today that he is following in his father's footsteps, the footsteps of the great Torah scholar, the Kronitzer Rebbe, Reb Moshe Yechezkel." Yankeleh was embarrassed by the thunderous acclamation of his father's Chassidim when they pounded their agreement on their *shtenders*. He felt undeserving of their acclaim.

A waft of the sweet-scented air of early spring brought him back to the present. "Moshe, do you remember how you felt the first time you were counted in the *minyan*?"

Moshe nodded, a smile lighting up his face. "I'll never forget that feeling, Yankeleh. Whenever I think about it I shiver. Believe me when I tell you that it was the greatest day in my life," he replied.

"I think I know how you felt," Yankeleh said. "Yesterday when I walked into the *shul* the *shammas* called out, 'Now we can begin, here comes our tenth man.' I turned to look behind me...and then the men called to me, and I realized that I was the tenth man."

The two friends laughed, reliving it all with pleasure.

"I have to admit something to you Moshe. I hope you'll forgive me," Yankeleh said. "But these past few months I have been terribly jealous of you. There I was seated next to my father, a little boy, and there you were, my older friend Moshe, important, counted in the *minyan*. I can't tell you how miserable I felt."

Moshe grinned sheepishly. "Six months older isn't that much older," he chided. "Besides, you don't have to apologize, Yankeleh. I felt the same way when Leibel Krinsky was bar mitzvah last year. After he was bar mitzvah, Leibel hardly looked at me. I guess he figured he didn't want to have anything to do with a little boy."

"To tell you the truth, I was afraid that you would ignore me, too, after you were bar mitzvah," Yankeleh admitted shyly, "that you wouldn't want to be friends with a `little boy.' "

"Not be your friend?" Moshe exclaimed, his brow wrinkling in astonishment. "But Yankeleh, I am honored that you count me as your friend. I mean, you...you are an *ilui* and the son of the Rebbe."

Yankeleh shook his head. "I am no different from anyone else. And I don't like to be called an *ilui*," he said, his tone reproving. "Aren't we friends because we like each other?"

"Of course. But you are still very special, and well..." He threw his hands up in exasperation, amazed at his friend's modesty.

Their conversation was halted by the sound of shrieks coming from the home of Avrum the cobbler. They exchanged glances.

"What was that?" Moshe asked.

Yankeleh swallowed hard. His hands suddenly felt clammy. "It sounds like something terrible is happening. Maybe we should get some help?"

"But it could be just a family argument: We would look foolish. Let's go see first."

They rushed in the direction of the shouts, then crept into the dark alley behind the cobbler's house.

"Can you see anything?" Yankeleh whispered breathlessly.

"Yes. I see the outline of men and a cart. Maybe they're thieves?"

"Shh, not so loud. If they see us…"

"Let's get closer," Moshe urged.

"I still can't see…"

A blow to his head left the sentence unfinished. The last words Yankeleh heard were, "Yoineh, we've got two more."

✳   ✳   ✳

The sergeant never hid his feelings of repugnance for the *khappers*—Yoineh Kloptschik the *ganav*, Velvel Shmuckler the horse thief, and Shmulik Shlagger the gambler. But the *kahal* had hired these men, and they were useful and had to be tolerated. He stood in front of the barracks, hands on hips, eyeing the three men suspiciously.

"What d'ya got there today? No more sick babies, you hear? The two yids you brought in last week died before I could even spit on them."

Velvel Shmuckler snickered. "Ah, come on Ivan, we get you some good *schoirah*, real good stuff. Listen, these kids are frail. What d'ya expect?"

"All right, all right, so what's in the cart today?"

The *khappers* had been so busy drinking, in celebration of their unexpectedly good catch, that they hadn't bothered looking at the boys since tying them together the night before. It was Yoineh who first realized their error: When he opened the cart and recognized the frightened boys, he grabbed his head, stuttering and gesticulating wildly.

"*Gevalt*, what did we do? We made a mistake, a terrible mistake."

"What are you blubbering about?" Ivan barked. "What mistake?"

"Listen, Ivan, take those two boys, the one with the curly hair and the one with the cross eye. The other two we gotta take back. But we promise you—on our mothers' heads—tomorrow you get four in their place."

"What the devil is this all about?" the sergeant shouted, his face florid with rage. "What kind of a game you got going here? Leave the goods like always and get out of my sight!"

The three *khappers* fidgeted nervously, exchanging gloomy looks. Shmulik Shlagger, the wiliest of the three, threw an arm around the sergeant.

"Ivan, we have a little problem here. It was pitch black, and we couldn't see who we grabbed. Now these two boys, well, their fathers are men of prominence. We don't want to get in trouble in the village. You understand?"

The sergeant leered at Shmulik, thrusting a finger in his face. "We ain't fussy here. We take all comers. You got problems with your Jews, that's your headache. I ain't sending anyone back."

"My noble friend, let me explain," Shmulik pleaded. "That tall boy, the one with the dark eyes, he's the son of the Kronitzer Rebbe. And the redhead, he's the son of the *gabbai*, also an important person."

Shmulik realized that his words were making no impression on the sergeant. After a moment's thought, he took the plunge.

"You leave it to us and we'll fill your pockets with rubles for these boys. What do you say?"

The sergeant screwed up his face in thought. "You bring the money and then we'll see. In the meantime, they stay here."

"Sure, you'll have it tomorrow. First thing. I promise."

By morning the entire village of Kronitz Podolsk was in turmoil. As the news of the kidnapping spread, pandemonium broke loose. The wails of the Rebbetzin could be heard throughout the village, piercing the hearts of even the most hardened. The Rebbe was haggard from a sleepless night spent reciting *tehillim* with only the *gabbai* at his side. He remained secluded in his home, swaying and rocking in prayer, his eyes raw with his own personal pain and with the pain he felt for all the children of Israel. Not a word had been exchanged between the two men throughout the long, terrible night.

The narrow lanes of the village were soon choked

by men wrapped in prayer shawls, their eyes turned heavenward, as they beseeched the *Ribono Shel Olam* to show mercy. Their prayers were matched by those of their wives, who stood wringing their hands and weeping, as children clutched their skirts, frightened by the strange doings. Though the years had brought anguish and evil decrees to these Jews, the news that their Rebbe's only son—their future leader, of whom they were already so proud—had been snatched away lent a sharper edge to their suffering.

It was a menacing crowd that greeted the terrified *khappers* when their cart rumbled into the village. Baruch Feinsilver, a prosperous merchant and representative of the *kahal,* was the first to step forward. The *khappers* clambered down from the cart, prepared to disclaim any involvement. But Feinsilver's angry face weakened their resolve.

The men began pleading, explaining that it had all been a mistake, a terrible error, and that all would be resolved with a few rubles. The quick-thinking Shmulik even promised to contribute money from their own pockets toward the freeing of the boys. All that was needed, he assured Feinsilver, was enough money to soften the heart of the sergeant in charge.

Feinsilver looked hard at the men. "You'll have the money within the hour," he barked. "And for your own sakes, you had better hope that no harm comes to our Yankeleh."

Yankeleh pulled the ragged blanket about him, but

the damp straw he was lying on provided no warmth, and he continued to shiver. They had been issued rough, olive-colored uniforms after their own clothes were thrown into a heap and burned before their eyes. It had been a day of threats and beatings, all to the cadence of Sergeant Ivan Zinoviev's shouted commands. By nightfall they were bruised in body and spirit, and their stomachs grumbled from gnawing hunger. Yankeleh licked his dry lips as he fought to contain his fear. Though exhausted, he tried to avoid closing his eyes and seeing the specter of his parents' tortured faces. Knowing their grief distressed him far more than anything he had endured that day. When sleep finally did come it was filled with nightmares.

They were awakened at first light by shouts and the butt of a rifle bruising their bare feet. The boys were shoved into a courtyard and ordered to undress and wash in the icy water of the outdoor cistern. Yankeleh took a deep breath and plunged his head into the water. Whoever hesitated for even one moment was lifted bodily and thrown into the cistern, feet and hands flailing from the shock of the bruising cold.

There were twenty boys in all, most of them thin, undernourished waifs from impoverished homes. Now their purple lips matched the veins drawn starkly on their shivering bodies. They huddled together in fright as the butt of the corporal's rifle urged them back into the barracks. Yankeleh saw from their size and appearance that the boys ranged in age from eight to twelve. The two boys from his own village, Itzik Shusterman and Shaya Melitzky, the cobbler's son, he knew to be no more than nine or ten.

He realized that he and Moshe were the oldest.

Once in the barracks, Yankeleh pulled the rough uniform over his damp body, glad for whatever warmth the cavernous room offered. He and Moshe quietly but fervently davened *Shacharis*. When he reached to tighten *tefillin* straps that weren't there, Yankeleh felt a pain in his heart; for the first time his courage almost failed him. Only the words of the *Shema* saved him from breaking down and weeping.

A cry of relief echoed through the room when a cauldron of steaming liquid was finally rolled in. Their teeth chattering, the boys pressed against each other, eager to be first in line to receive a ladle of gruel and a piece of stale black bread.

Only Yankeleh held back. This food was undoubtedly cooked by a non-Jew in *treif* pots. How could he eat such a thing? But if he refused, he would starve. It was clearly a matter of *pikuach nefesh*, life and death. He would eat, he decided, but only enough to sustain him. And he would never, never let actual *treif* meat pass his lips, not if his ordeal lasted a lifetime. With set lips and determined brow, Yankeleh slowly put the spoon to his mouth.

After gobbling down his meager portion, Moshe made his way over to Yankeleh. "What are we going to do? How can we run away from here?" he blubbered, the tears rolling down his cheeks.

Yankeleh's jaw tightened. He had to encourage his friend, to give him hope. "Listen to me, Moshe. We're older than the other boys here and we have to set an example for them. We have to be brave, to give them courage not to surrender to the beatings and threats. If they see us cave in, all is lost," Yankeleh said grimly.

"I…I don't know," Moshe stuttered. "I'm not as brave as you are."

"No one is born brave, Moshe, but we have to pretend that we aren't afraid of them. The bruises will heal, but if we bend to their will then our souls will never recover. We will be torn from our faith, from our people. It will be the end of everything we believe in, everything that we hold sacred. You know what they have in mind for us, Moshe. *Chas ve'shalom* that we should lose our *emunah*. We must be prepared to offer our very lives for *kiddush Hashem*. Try to remember Rabbi Akiva," he said.

Moshe gasped at the specter of martyrdom. His voice became an agonized plea. "Maybe our families will ransom us?"

Yankeleh cast an apprehensive glance at his friend. "Yes," he said, "I am sure they will try."

It was mid-afternoon by the time Baruch Feinsilver's carriage rolled into the courtyard of the Nikolayev canton, the three *khappers* accompanying him on horseback. Huffing, he pulled his thickset body from the well-appointed carriage and entered the barracks.

A surly Sergeant Ivan Alexeivich Zinoviev awaited them. Seated pompously behind a weathered desk, he scoured the faces of the men before him with contempt. Only Baruch was offered a chair. The *khappers* stood awkwardly behind him. The introductions were swift and lacking in courtesy.

"What brings so honored a guest here?" the sergeant

grunted, affecting ignorance of the purpose of the visit.

Baruch cleared his throat. "We understand, sir, that a grave error has occurred and that two boys from our village, both from prestigious families, were accidentally brought here. The arrangement we have with these men," he continued, indicating the three standing at uncomfortable attention, "is as you know, to…to…" he stammered in search of a euphemism, "to supply the Czar with boys from poor families who would benefit from the free education provided in the cantons," he concluded with a sigh, pleased with his tactful turn of phrase.

The sergeant grinned ominously. "We know nothing of your internal arrangements, Mr. Feinsilver. Such arrangements are left completely in your hands. Our concern here is only that each community provide the cantons with the quota of boys assigned to it," he said, his phrases polished for the sake of his guest. "The Czar has complete faith in the *kahals,*" he said with a cynical smirk, "and he knows that you will not disappoint him and that the quotas will be met. Now you tell me that you want two lads returned to the village?"

Baruch fidgeted nervously. He nodded, and drew out a packet, which he placed in front of the sergeant. "Naturally we wish to show our appreciation for your cooperation. We are aware that this is an unusual request."

The sergeant eyed the packet hungrily, but Baruch Feinsilver and the *khappers* could not know that Sergeant Zinoviev's shrewdness far exceeded even his personal greed. He had already reported the incident to a senior officer, who had then discussed the matter with Bishop Feodor Gargarin. The sergeant opened the packet without ceremony and counted out the rubles, his face devoid of expression. Replacing the rubles in the packet he nodded to the corporal. Within minutes a whimpering Moshe Vohlman was presented to the waiting delegation.

Baruch felt his chest tightening. "Where is the other boy?" he asked in a guttural whisper.

"You get only this one," the sergeant snarled. "Take him or leave him."

Baruch shuddered. His eyes narrowing, he surveyed the faces of the *khappers*. "But I was led to understand… that is, it was made clear that the ransom was for two boys. There is a small fortune in that packet," he hissed.

The sergeant jumped to his feet, his face growing livid. "If you know what's good for you, Jew, you'll leave now. I can change my mind about this one, too."

They stalked from the room, Baruch mumbling curses under his breath. Without so much as a word of sympathy, he led Moshe into his carriage. He sighed deeply, mopping the beads of perspiration running down his face and neck.

TWO

IN THE DIM LIGHT of dawn, Yankeleh heard the massive door of the barracks clang open. He held his breath as the huge corporal heaved a squirming burlap bag onto the barracks floor and lumbered out. Four dazed boys crawled out from their burlap prison. The clamor wakened the others. Shaking their heads they murmured their sympathy at the sight of the frightened newcomers, who sat huddled together like a tattered bundle of rags, their eyes filled with terror. Forcing a smile, Yankeleh approached them first.

"Where are you from?" he asked.

"From Kirov."

"All of you?"

They nodded their heads affirmatively.

"Do you know where you are?"

The boys exchanged glances, then nodded solemnly.

One boy, the smallest, with huge, porcelain blue eyes now brimming with tears, edged closer. "My mamma told me about the *khappers* and the cantons," he whimpered. "They're going to make us *goyim*," he sniffled, wiping his tears with dirt-stained hands.

Yankeleh patted the child's head. "What's your name?" he asked gently.

"Alter Sholom," he sputtered, rubbing the tears that edged their way down his cheek.

"And how old are you, Alter Sholom?"

"On Shavuos I'll be nine."

"Are all of you the same age?"

"I'm ten," one lad called out.

"And the rest of you?"

"Eleven," the remaining replied in unison.

By then the other conscripts had gathered about, shaking their heads sorrowfully at the new victims.

Yankeleh surveyed the forlorn faces of the new conscripts, his heart smarting with pain for them. He knew that it was more than pity that he was feeling—it was a gnawing feeling of despair that came from the very depth of his soul. Why was this happening? Why was he being tortured like this?

He looked at tiny Alter Sholom, gazing at him with terrified eyes, seeking comfort, and suddenly the horror of the past few weeks began to wear another aspect. Perhaps *Hakadosh Baruch Hu* wanted him to be with these children at this terrible time. A sense of awe swept over him, and for the first time, Yankeleh knew there was purpose in his suffering. The *Ribono Shel Olam* was testing him. He now understood his role: He was to serve as a source of courage for these desolate children. But setting an example would not be enough. He had to find a way to inspire these children, to give them hope, and to strengthen their devotion to Torah so that they would survive all adversity that the future held.

Buoyed with his new mission, Yankeleh could not know how fraught with danger the road ahead would be.

"We old-timers will help you the best we can," he reassured them. "Just remember, right now do what the sergeant and the corporal tell you to do. Don't cry and don't answer back," he warned. "Try to avoid angering those monsters. Don't give them a reason to beat you."

Yankeleh took a deep breath and drew himself upright. "Boys, there is only one chance for survival, the most important kind of survival, survival of the spirit. The only way we can hope to defeat the *sonei Yisrael*—who want to tear us from our faith—is by knowledge, by learning. This is our secret strength, our greatest weapon. Through learning we can overcome fear and despair. If you are willing, I can teach you."

The children exchanged wary looks. Ten-year-old Huna Schiffman, one of the new boys, shook his head, sniffling and pulling his earlock.

"But we have no books. They took everything from us, even the Chumash and Siddur my father gave me."

"You won't need books. I can teach you without them."

There was a hum as the voices of the earlier conscripts

rose and fell in animated discussion. Reuven Fenster, who was nearing bar mitzvah age, was pushed forward.

"Yankeleh," he said, looking away nervously, obviously uncomfortable in his new role of spokesman, "Itzik and Shaya from your village say that you are an *ilui*. Is that true?"

Yankeleh reddened. But the hopeful look in Reuven's eyes erased his embarrassment.

"People do call me that," he admitted uncomfortably. "I suppose it's because I have a good memory. You see, I know many Gemara tractates by heart…and the Chumash as well." He blushed, unaccustomed to making such boasts, but seeing the impact of his words, he forced himself to continue. "You see, Reuven, it's all up here," he said, pointing to his head, "and here," pointing to his heart. "No matter what they do, they can't take the Torah away from me. And that goes for all of you—the more you know, the stronger you will be. Just remember that our Torah is our *schoirah* and that no matter where we are we take that *schoirah* with us. Every one of us is a link in the chain that leads back to Avraham Avinu. We can't let them break that chain, can we? No matter what they say, or what they do to us, remember that we are Jews, and that *Hakadosh Baruch Hu* made a covenant with His people, which began with Avraham and was renewed at Sinai. And don't forget our redemption from Egyptian bondage by the Almighty. If you are willing to learn, then that chain will never be broken. It will be forged with steel and bonded in our souls. And the Almighty will redeem us from this bondage, too."

The boys stared at him with open mouths.

"When can we begin?" Reuven said slowly.

Yankeleh smiled. "Reuven, we just began."

It was several days later that the sergeant announced that their "religions" tutor, Father Igor Grodno, had arrived. Benches were lined up, and they were seated in neat rows to await what they all feared most.

Father Grodno was a large man, with a wild thatch of black beard that cascaded down to the top of his silver crucifix. His expression was fierce as his first words came thundering out of his mouth.

"You are all damned," he shouted, pointing a long, knobby finger at them. "You are all damned to eternal hell. And do you know why?"

The boys shivered, too terrified to move.

"Because you killed our savior, and you are damned to eternal hell, damned forever to be enslaved, to wander the world without a home. But I am here to save you, to mold and reshape you so that your little souls will find salvation in the true faith."

He waved a leather-bound New Testament before them, his eyes glowing with fervor. "How fortunate you are that our Czar loves you so much and cares for you so deeply that he is giving you this holy Bible as a gift. I warn you, take good care of this precious gift, and tomorrow we will discuss the Gospel according to Matthew. Tonight you are to read this Gospel. I expect correct answers tomorrow," he said ominously. "And those of

you who can't read Russian, have a friend read to you."
He then beckoned for Yankeleh to step forward. Much to
Yankeleh's astonishment the priest placed both his hands
on his shoulders, drawing him closer to him. "So you are
the son of a rebbe, a wonder worker perhaps?"

Yankeleh replied quietly, his eyes avoiding the stern
gaze of the prelate, "I am the son of the Kronitzer Rebbe, a
man of great learning and piety, but not a miracle maker.
For if he were, I surely would not be here today."

The priest laughed. "Indeed, indeed," he exclaimed
with a wry smile. "But you know that your father is in
league with the devil!" he said. "And you, my son, will
have the chance to expiate the sins of your father, and
your father's father."

Yankeleh blanched. "My father is a man of God," he
replied, meeting the priest's gaze. "He has never harmed
another human being, nor has he ever sinned against
man or God. There are no sins to be expiated for my
father or for my grandfather, who was a *tzaddik*."

The priest struck Yankeleh sharply across the face,
his ring cutting Yankeleh's lip. Yankeleh flinched, then
swallowed hard.

"My father is not a sinner," he shouted, steeling
himself for the next blow.

"I admire filial loyalty," the priest whispered, his
voice now cajoling, though Yankeleh saw the fury in his
eyes, which burned like fiery coals. "Tomorrow, Yaakov,
you will recite the first five pages of the assigned Gospel
by heart. And remember, the punishment for anyone
who cannot answer questions will be swift and painful,"

he said, pointing to the whip in Corporal Yusopovich's hand. "Today we have been charitable, but our Christian charity ends tomorrow. And surely the son of a rebbe reads Russian? So it will be your task, Yaakov, to read the Gospels to those who aren't fluent in our beautiful language, as I know you to be."

For a split second Yankeleh stood mute. He then shook his head no.

"You mean you won't read?" the priest asked menacingly, his eyes narrowing.

"I can't read Russian, sir," he replied, his eyes wide with innocence. "I can speak Russian and Ukrainian, but I have never been taught to read these languages, sir."

The color of the priest's face darkened. He folded his hands and pursed his lips. "I see that our little scholar is modest. I suggest that you search your mind carefully for the Russian alphabet, Yaakov, son of the Kronitzer Rebbe," he growled, "for tomorrow you will be tested on the Gospel I have assigned. And I expect you all to know the correct answers. All the answers," he snapped, stalking out of the room.

Yankeleh looked at the children and saw the terror on their faces. He wondered how he could possibly succeed. For the past few days he had been reviewing basics with them. He would daven with them, and then review the blessings recited before and after meals.

He spent much time on the *halachos* of Shabbos, suggesting ways in which at least the most basic forms of *melachah* could be avoided, and assuring the boys that in the life-and-death situation that they now found themselves in, the Shabbos desecration that they might be forced into was permissible.

He spoke to them of *mesiras nefesh*, of sacrifice, and of the reward that awaited them in the World to Come. Now Yankeleh feared that all of his efforts would be destroyed with the first slash of the whip. There had to be a way to outwit this evil that threatened to destroy them. But how? For the moment he would maintain that he could not read Russian, which, as the prelate suspected, was not true. The Rebbe had long ago engaged tutors to teach Yankeleh to read and write both Russian and Ukrainian. He had explained to Yankeleh that it was of great importance for a rebbe to be fluent in both languages because there were times when a rebbe had to intervene with the Russian government on his people's behalf. A rebbe also had to read and understand all of the proclamations and laws issued by the Czar.

"May *Hashem Yisborach* help me to be strong," he prayed.

Early the next morning, the boys lined up on the benches to await Father Grodno. They sat forlornly, dread on their faces. Through the door they could hear snatches of the priest's conversation with Sergeant Zinoviev. Yankeleh's name was repeated several times. The boys stared gloomily at Yankeleh. Yankeleh sat expressionless, appearing not to notice their stares.

Father Grodno had delayed his lesson for good reason. The Bishop had given special instructions about Yaakov Yitzchak Halevi, and he now shared the plan with the sergeant, who shook his head in doubtful agreement.

"Do you know why the Church refused to ransom that one?" the priest asked.

The sergeant shrugged.

"The Bishop has great plans for him. When little Yaakov bends to our will—and is baptized—he will serve as an example for all the others to follow. Ah, yes, the Bishop is very pleased that this one fell into our hands."

"But I can tell you he is no easy mark," the sergeant put in. "How do you plan to break him?"

A malicious grin creased the priest's face. "You can depend on the Church, Ivan. We have our ways. He will see the light. Of that I have no doubt." He strode into the barracks.

Father Grodno greeted the boys with a smile of satisfaction still on his face, but the smile turned to a scowl as he stared at the rows of conscripts before him.

"Now my little yids, I hope you all enjoyed your reading assignment," he said.

He began asking his questions. First he pointed to Itzik, who rose and declared that he could not read Russian. He was answered by a swift stroke of the lash. As each child rose and made the same declaration, the lash struck out across his frail back.

The prelate turned to Yankeleh.

"So Yaakov, did you find your Russian alphabet?"

"I tried, sir," he said, shaking his head, "but the letters refused to reveal themselves to me."

"Beware of your tone of voice, Yaakov. You are

bordering on the insolent."

Yankeleh lowered his eyes dutifully and with a show of humility continued. "Sir, I beg you to consider that these boys can barely speak Russian or Ukrainian. To expect them to understand a text in a tongue foreign to them is unreasonable."

"Ah, yes. You do have a point there, Yaakov. But then again, you know how to read Russian."

"Only to speak the language, sir," he said once again. "I can be of little help, sir."

"Well, then, do you want to set a fine example for the rest of the lads? An example that will make my task and their lot easier?"

"If I can, sir."

"Good. Then kneel and kiss the crucifix."

The conscripts gasped.

Yankeleh replied. "Sir, that I cannot do. It is against my religious belief to bow before anyone but the Lord, our God."

No sooner had he uttered these words when the now enraged priest motioned for the corporal to strip him. Yankeleh was thrown on the floor. He gritted his teeth, admonishing himself not to make a sound. The lash ripped through his flesh, cutting deep, until the rivulets of blood pooled about him. Only then did the prelate indicate that the flogging should stop. The corporal yanked an almost unconscious Yankeleh to his feet and pushed him toward the priest.

"We do not enjoy meting out such harsh punishment,

but you leave me little choice. Now Yaakov, think carefully. You are an intelligent lad. Is your life of so little value that you are willing to forfeit it so easily? And what of the lives of the other boys? Have you no compassion for them? If you come to us, they will follow. Don't let them die because of your false pride and stubbornness. You now have the chance to become a true Russian, a son of the Russian Orthodox Church. Agree to baptism and your lot will be eased. If not, you will feel the lash on your back until the very breath of life will be flogged from you. Make your choice now, Yaakov. Kneel and kiss the cross."

Yankeleh opened his mouth as if to reply, but his knees buckled, and he fainted at the feet of the priest.

A vat filled with grease had been left for the boys to rub as a salve into their wounds. They agreed that Reuven, the eldest among them, would rub the healing salve on Yankeleh's raw back. Reuven approached Yankeleh, his hands trembling, knowing full well that every touch would cause great pain to a beloved friend.

He crouched beside Yankeleh and whispered in his ear. "Yankeleh, dear friend, please forgive me, for what I have to do now will be very painful," he murmured, "but if I don't rub the salve on your wounds, they won't heal. Please forgive me," he pleaded, "but it must be done." Very carefully he applied the salve, wincing at Yankeleh's moans.

When sleep finally drew Yankeleh from his pain, it was not a sleep that brought him rest. Instead, the monstrous faces of his torturers danced before him, taunting him. He cried out, trying to escape from the horrible vision. And then he saw his father standing before him, his sad eyes shining with pride.

"Yankeleh, my dear son, how I suffer with you," his father said in a soft voice. "But know that the pain you suffer is fleeting; it will pass. By your example you are heartening these poor children, and saving them from committing a terrible sin. Stand firm in your faith. Your suffering will seem like nothing if you keep in mind the martyrdom of Channah and her sons. Remember the words of Rabbi Akiva, `Just as a fish cannot live outside of water, so the Jewish people cannot live outside of Torah.' And never forget the last words on his lips as he was flayed alive: `Hear, O Israel, the Lord is our God, the Lord is One.' My son, as the lash tears at you turn your thoughts to Rabbi Akiva, who welcomed his martyrdom at the hands of the Romans, so that he could fulfill the biblical command: `And you shall love the Lord your God with all of your heart, and all of your soul, and all of your might.' "

Yankeleh awoke in a feverish sweat, his body trembling. Now he knew beyond the shadow of a doubt that he was on the right path and that he would prevail. His father's words had tempered his body and his soul, and he was ready to meet the afflictions that lay ahead. He would not succumb—not to threats, not to the lash. He heaved a sigh and fell into a peaceful sleep.

It took Yankeleh a week to recover from his wounds, and though he was again forced to submit to Father Grodno's questioning, for the present there were no more lashings. But that peace did not last long. A month after Yankeleh had been nearly flogged to death, Huna Schiffman died from a combination of mistreatment and malnutrition. What the beatings and the floggings could not achieve, the death of Huna did. Both Itzik Shusterman and Shaya Melitzky accepted baptism. The rewards of their baptism were two clean cots and clean uniforms. Nor were they required to stand in line for meager food rations. Corporal Yusopovich brought them platters filled with meats and vegetables. Yankeleh observed with growing fear how the ill-treated children looked with envy upon the two boys, renamed Alexei and Sasha.

He now worked feverishly with the other boys, reviewing what he had already taught and delving ever deeper in a frantic attempt to enrich their knowledge. He consoled them with reassurances that Huna would now receive his reward in *Olam HaBa*. But the hunger pangs could not be ignored, and their tender years weakened their resolve. When ten year old Shaya Eisenstein chose to be baptized, Yankeleh wept through the night.

Father Grodno had given Yankeleh a respite, no doubt out of fear of having almost killed his prize, and now he was ready to renew his efforts. This time the wily priest changed his tactics. Instead of threatening him, he invited Yankeleh to sit with him and discuss religion, taunting him with, "Maybe you will be able to convince me to become a Jew."

Although Yankeleh came to fear their discussions, which were in fact disputations, he did remarkably well against the aging priest, whose own knowledge of Judaism, even Bible, was weak. After weeks of futile dialogue, the priest returned to his original style: After a particularly grueling debate, one in which Yankeleh clearly bested him, the priest ordered the boy to be flogged for mocking the Church. This time the wounds did not heal so readily. Feverish, Yankeleh was sent to the nearest hospital, where for the first time in six months he slept in a bed and drank warm, fresh milk. Alas, this sorely needed rest was to last for less than a week.

By November, the barracks had turned into an icy cavern. Although the rations were increased to two bowls of soup and a bowl of gruel each day, it was not enough to sustain the children. Malnutrition and cold joined forces with pneumonia, and before winter's arrival Lazar Shonberg, Yisrael Katzenellenbogen, and Haskel Duvid Koren were no longer among the living.

When the orders arrived for the conscripts to leave the canton, sixteen boys were left from the original twenty-four. The *meshumadim*, the ones who had been baptized, had long before been taken from Nikolayev to parts unknown.

One icy morning in December the boys were awakened before dawn and placed in the charge of the vicious Corporal Yusopovich and two privates. They were forced to march behind a cart carrying the soldiers. With tears freezing on their icy cheeks, the conscripts stumbled forward, wrapped in khaki blankets, their shoes stuffed with rags to keep their feet from freezing. In the dead of winter they marched eastward, their heads and bodies bowed before the gale force winds.

THREE

YANKELEH DID HIS best to encourage the flagging boys. He stopped to lift those who dropped to their knees from exhaustion, and at one point carried Alter Sholom on his shoulders until the child regained enough strength to walk on his own. They had marched a distance of twelve miles when, with dusk falling, Corporal Yusopovich halted in front of an inn.

After negotiating with the innkeeper, the boys were herded into a barn. Yankeleh knew that the three guards would soon be drunk and would surely forget about the starving conscripts. He called up all of his courage and approached the corporal.

"Sir," he pleaded, "we have not eaten all day."

The corporal spat at Yankeleh. "Aren't you yids used to fasting? So, fast! Too much food ain't all that good for you brats."

Yankeleh blinked away the gathering tears. He was prepared to throw himself at the monster's feet to get some food for the children, but miraculously that was not necessary. No sooner had the corporal spoken than the two privates began to argue with him. Yankeleh heard the private called Volya insist that the boys at least be given some bread. Then, ignoring the corporal, the soldier stomped into the inn and minutes later brought out a sack filled with stale bread, which he handed to Yankeleh.

Yankeleh's expression of gratitude said more than words. The boys huddled together, snuggling closer to the animals for warmth. The horses grew nervous, pawing the ground and whinnying. The cows became restless. But Yankeleh and the children were indifferent to the tumult about them, all their thoughts on the stale bread—try as they would, they could not make a dent in the bread's crust. There seemed to be no way of making it edible. The children began whimpering.

"Why are they doing this to us? For what purpose?"

"The reasons are clear, Reuven. Only too clear," Yankeleh answered.

"But what's the purpose of kidnapping children if they mean to kill us? Why go to all of the trouble of starving and torturing us first?"

"Their plan for us is no different than those of our enemies throughout our history; to beat their religion into us." Yankeleh said. "If we accept baptism, they've gained another Russian soldier devoted to the Czar and their Church. The *meshumadim* are sent off to slave for some peasant or for the army. They are watched carefully to prevent a return to *Yiddishkeit*. Then at the age of eighteen, off to the army for twenty-five years. They have woven a tight net for us fish," he whispered bitterly.

"Their problem begins when we don't follow their plan. Then what's left for them to do but to thin out the ranks without having to actually kill us. You know—why waste good food on Jews? Starvation will do the job just as well.

"This march is supposed to either soften us up or kill us. If, by some miracle, we manage to survive, well, they'll devise something else. But Reuven, we have to have faith that with God's help we will overcome. *Hashem* is always with us—they can't take that away from us."

Reuven moaned, "We'll starve to death, Yankeleh. The bread is too hard to eat."

Yankeleh leaned forward, his head in his hands. Then, as if struck by lightning, he jumped to his feet. "Anyone here know how to milk a cow?" he called out.

"I…I do," Simchaleh Wachsman, pale and shivering, mumbled.

"Good. There's a pail over in the corner."

"I think that the cow in the corner has milk," Simchaleh said. "But…but cows don't like strangers. She could kick the bucket."

Yankeleh slipped his arm through Simchaleh's and gave him a gentle, encouraging shove. "Now Simchaleh, you know how to talk to a cow, don't you?"

For the first time that day, the children smiled.

Simchaleh Wachsman edged gingerly over to the cow. Patting her flanks, he whispered words of reassurance. She turned her head away disdainfully and snorted. He cast a side long glance at the boys, now waiting eagerly for Simchaleh to make progress in his negotiations. Once again he patted her flank, then moved closer to her head and whispered in her ear. With great caution he set the stool near her udders and slowly began milking. At first only a dribble of milk trickled into the bucket, but as he grew more assured a frothy white stream filled it. With great care he got up from the stool and backed away from the cow's side, cradling the precious bucket to his chest.

The boys sent up a cheer as they scrambled forward. Only Yankeleh's sharp reprimand prevented the milk from being spilled by the hunger-crazed children. Yankeleh took the bread and soaked it in the warm milk, then handed out the softened bread to the children and recited the *brachah* with them. They munched hungrily, the milk dribbling down their chins. When not even a crust of bread was left, Yankeleh passed around the bucket of rich, nourishing milk.

Reuven looked at Yankeleh in wonder. "That was a stroke of genius," he exclaimed.

"And now let's pray that the *Ribono Shel Olam* will continue to provide us with sustenance," Yankeleh exclaimed, reminding the boys that it was time to *bentch*.

The children awoke in the morning to rays of sunshine streaming through the slats of the barn. The corporal's gruff command prodded them to their feet.

Before they began the day's march, Yankeleh had them stuff straw into their clothing for extra warmth. The rest and food had restored their flagging spirits, and throughout the morning Yankeleh and Reuven kept their morale high by singing *nigunim*. But by midday the pale sun faded, and the snow began to fall.

Yankeleh walked behind Alter Sholom. He was struggling manfully to keep pace with the others, but as the day wore on he began to stumble. Yankeleh and Reuven took turns hoisting him onto their shoulders, but neither of them had the strength to carry the featherweight child very far. When at last they reached a tavern for the night, the boys plodded into the barn, too exhausted to eat the dried bread left for them.

In the black of night, Yankeleh heard a cry and then gasps. His body tense, all his senses alerted, he groped toward the sound. He found Avrumchik Feigenbaum doubled over, gasping and coughing, and Mordechai Aaron Mandelstam too weak to even lift his head. Avrumchik and Mordechai Aaron had been inseparable from the moment they met in the Nikolayev canton. For days Yankeleh had been listening to their coughing with growing apprehension. He had even pleaded with the corporal to have pity and let the sick boys travel on the cart, only to have his plea met with a wad of spittle and a curse. Now he could only comfort them by reciting *tehillim* and caressing their burning brows with his cool hand. They finally dropped into a peaceful sleep. The next morning they didn't wake up. Yankeleh closed their eyes and recited *Kaddish* over them.

When Yankeleh and Reuven reported their death,

the corporal cackled, "Two less scurvy animals to feed." He handed the tavern owner a few rubles to bury the boys, while Yankeleh begged for the children to be given a Jewish burial.

"Why do you waste your breath trying to find some humanity in that pig?" Reuven cried out in a fury. The corporal's riding crop slashed Reuven's cheek, barely missing his eye. Yankeleh gasped and pulled Reuven away from the infuriated corporal.

That morning's march began in a light drizzle, which soon turned to punishing sleet. Even the horses were reluctant to travel. It was still early in the afternoon when the corporal headed to the closest village. Not a soul was to be seen when the cart clattered in front of the inn, which was boarded up against the elements. The corporal pounded long and hard at the door before the innkeeper peered out.

"We need food and lodgings for the night," the corporal barked.

"Yes, yes, come in. Forgive the appearance. We don't have too many guests at this time of year. Now, how many boys do you have?"

Ignoring the question, the corporal growled, "You got a barn?"

"Yes, yes, of course, in the back."

"Good. Throw these yids into it."

The innkeeper cast a baleful glance at the boys. "The barn is in poor repair. It's really falling apart. I can find room for the lads here."

"You want this lice-infested bunch in your inn?"

The innkeeper shrugged his shoulders.

"Well I don't want them here with me. You don't want them in the barn. Then let them sleep outside—it's all the same to me."

The innkeeper scurried out and told the boys to follow him. The barn was in fact warm and clean, and the shivering boys clapped their hands and stomped their feet to regain lost circulation. Without saying a word, the innkeeper rushed away to attend to his three guests.

Yankeleh had concealed the uneaten bread from the night before and he was about to check the cows for milk when the barn door squeaked open. The shadowy light of the lantern revealed the motherly face of a woman. Her expression froze as she surveyed the children, now sitting or lying on the straw. "*Guttenyu, Yiddishe kinder!* What do they want from our children?" she wailed. She wiped the tears from her cheeks, and with a finger to her lips, she motioned for them to follow her. The boys trudged behind her, exchanging uneasy glances. They were led into a large kitchen with a huge fire in the hearth. A Chanukah menorah graced a table near the window. The boys stared in open astonishment.

"We are in a Jewish home!" Yankeleh exclaimed joyously.

"Chanukah, it's Chanukah!" they all cried out.

The innkeeper soon joined them, his eyes brimming with unspoken emotion. "My name is Menashe Feigenbaum, and this is my wife, Raizel. And you boys are *nebech* cantonist children. Oy…" he sighed, "five boys from our own village were just taken away last week. What will be?" he said, throwing his hands in the air. "Listen, my children. The three soldiers are now fast asleep. I gave them enough vodka to keep them sleeping like babies for the night. Now go wash. There's plenty of hot water in those pans over there. Take off your wet clothes. I will give you blankets to keep you warm until your *shmattes* dry."

While her husband spoke, Raizel Feigenbaum scurried about preparing food. The smell of the sizzling latkes tantalized the children, who stood staring at her and sniffing the aroma.

"Reb Feigenbaum, how can we thank you for... for all of this?" Yankeleh stammered, blinking away the tears. "Please, is it possible for us to fulfill the mitzvah of lighting the menorah?"

"Yes, yes. I will ready the wicks for you." He looked into Yankeleh's thin face, studying the boy for a moment. "And who are you and where are you from?"

"Yaakov Yitzchak Halevi, from Kronitz Podolsk, sir."

The man looked stricken as he grasped the back of the chair. "You...you are not the Kronitzer Rebbe's son?"

A startled Yankeleh stared open-mouthed at Reb Feigenbaum. He nodded yes.

"*Gut in himmel*," the innkeeper exclaimed, "You are still alive, and not...not baptized?"

"*Chas v'chalilah*," Yankeleh cried, regaining his composure. "Do you know my family?"

"My dear child," he cried, embracing the boy. "I am

a Kronitzer Chassid, and I was at your *bris*. The news of your kidnapping was like Tishah B'Av for all of us—how we cried and prayed!" He then looked at the wan boy before him and blew his nose noisily. "We will write to your parents as soon as you finish eating. We must inform them that you are alive and well, and most important, that you remain a good and faithful Jew," he declared.

"My parents, are they well?" Yankeleh asked.

"Yes, my son, as well as one can be after such a terrible catastrophe. But as soon as they hear that you are alive and well...I don't have to tell you what this will mean to them."

Hearing the conversation, his wife rushed to her husband's side, her hands clasped to her breast as she stared in wonder at the boy in her kitchen. "Menashe, what are we to do? We can't let these boys go!"

"Mrs. Feigenbaum, I know you want to help us, but you can't hide all of us. The army would come and you and your whole family would be sent to prison. All we ask for is the chance to light the menorah and eat a warm meal."

Holding her white apron to her face, she shook her head in amazement.

The children washed in steaming hot water for the first time in months. Wrapped in clean blankets, they huddled about the menorah while Yankeleh lit the *shammas*.

His eyes closed, his voice hushed, he began. "Blessed are You, Lord our God, King of the universe, Who sanctified us with His commandments and commanded us to kindle the lights of Chanukah.

"Blessed are You, Lord our God, King of the universe, Who performed wondrous deeds for our fathers in the ancient days of this season.

"Blessed are You, Lord our God, King of the universe, Who has kept us alive, sustained us, and enabled us to reach this season."

With a trembling hand, he lit the prepared wicks as the others looked on breathlessly. When all eight wicks gave off their flickering lights, the children began to quietly sing, "*Maoz tzur yehshuosi…*" The innkeeper and his wife, standing nearby, wept openly.

For some minutes the children stood and watched the lights, dreaming dreams of their lost childhood.

As they noisily gathered around the kitchen table, Yankeleh warned everybody to eat slowly and not to overeat. Raizel assured them that she had packed enough food to last each one of them several days. The boys recited *HaMotzie* over warm, fresh bread, on which they spread a layer of chicken fat and *gribbenes*. They sank their forks into delicious, thick potato *latkes* followed by steaming bowls of soup. After an enthusiastic *bentching*, the Feigenbaums gave them pen and paper with which to write a few words to their parents, which the Feigenbaums would make sure were delivered to each and every father and mother. After the letters were carefully folded and placed in envelopes, the children gratefully fell onto the down quilts that had been piled in the corner for them. Within seconds they were fast asleep.

Before dawn they were awakened by Menashe Feigenbaum. "Children, dress quickly before the soldiers wake. You have to get back into the barn. They musn't know that you have been here or that we gave you food to take with you. Now come quickly."

The boys stumbled from the warmth of the kitchen into the bracing, icy air. They scuttled into the barn, bitterly recalling the reality of their situation.

Menashe motioned to Yankeleh. "I have spoken to the rabbi. And although this is a poor village, we are ready to offer these soldiers a ransom to let you go."

Yankeleh shook his head. "No, you mustn't make such an offer," he said. "They will never give me up. I'm some kind of a prize for them. But..." he grabbed the innkeeper's hands, "but you could save the life of Alter Sholom. Please, offer the ransom for him," he implored. "I beg you. The child will never survive this march. You could save his life."

The startled innkeeper shook his head uncertainly. "I don't think, well, I don't know if we could raise a ransom for...for another boy," he stammered.

Yankeleh stared at the embarrassed Jew. "Please," he pleaded, "I beg you, save a Jewish child, I beg you."

Menashe embraced the boy. "If that is your wish, Yankeleh, we will ransom Alter Sholom. This I vow."

Yankeleh did not reveal his conversation with the innkeeper to anyone for fear that the negotiations might fail. He began the morning prayers with the boys, rocking to and fro as he davened, delighting in the feel of the *tefillin* that he'd gratefully borrowed from the kindly innkeeper.

This time when the barn door was opened, instead of the corporal, a tall, grim faced Jew entered. Behind him stood the sullen soldiers.

"Which one of you is Yaakov Yitzchak Halevi?"

Yankeleh held his breath. He finally stepped forward. "I am Yaakov Yitzchak Halevi."

The older man stared at the young boy, his mouth quivering. "I am Rav Moshe Rosenthal, the rabbi of this village. I know your father from childhood days," he said. "Reb Menashe has told me of your request, and I understand the problem you and we face. I have spoken to the corporal, and for the sum we offered he has agreed to permit Alter Sholom to remain behind."

"I have no words for my gratitude. I thank you with all of my heart."

The austere-looking rabbi embraced the young man. "I shall write to your father immediately. Have no fear. Be strong, and remember that *Hashem* is watching over you. May He bless you and keep you, my dear son," he cried, pulling himself away.

Yankeleh found Alter Sholom curled up fast asleep. He lifted the sleeping child up and tenderly placed him in the rabbi's outstretched arms.

FOUR

THEY WERE WITHIN a day's march of Rostov when the gray weather turned into a thick blizzard. Rearing and whinnying, the horses refused to go farther. Corporal Yusopovich cracked his whip at their flanks and shouted curses. He had boasted that he would drag the conscripts to the army base in Rostov that day no matter how many dropped along the way. "Let them take care of you filthy yids. We did our job," he had cackled between deep swigs of vodka. Overhearing bits and pieces of conversation, Yankeleh judged that once in Rostov they would be marched northeast to some distant destination. It was obvious to Yankeleh that in addition to thinning out their ranks, the plan was to take them as far from home as possible.

But the best-laid plans of the corporal did not concern the team of four horses. They remained rooted in place, snorting noisily as they pawed the frozen ground, indifferent to curses and the whip. The desperate corporal jumped from the wagon. Patting the steeds' quivering flanks, his tone now conciliatory, he cajoled the horses to take them as far as the nearest village, promising that they, too, would get a good rest and plenty of water and oats. To the astonishment of the conscripts, the corporal's words calmed the steeds. Straining against the driven snow, the horses managed to regain their footing. Two hours later, horses and children plodded into the village of Petrovaskoy. To everyone's relief, a ramshackle inn loomed out of the haze. A drowsy innkeeper dashed out to greet his unexpected guests, but the sight of the half-frozen conscripts squelched his enthusiasm.

"Put these pigs in the barn," the corporal snorted, pointing to the haggard boys. Over the innkeeper's protests, the privates kicked and dragged the children into the adjacent barn. Later that evening, the innkeeper secretly brought them a huge pot of steaming kasha, but he found the children too weak to eat. More dead than alive, they lay scattered about like so many rag dolls. He crept away, shaking his head in compassion.

The night was bitter cold. The howling wind tore through the boards of the barn and clawed at the shivering children who were pressed together in a desperate search for warmth. Unable to sleep, Yankeleh leaned his head against the wall. He stared heavenward, as if his eyes could pierce the boards, and reached out to his Maker. In a low beseeching voice, Yankeleh poured out his heart, using the words of King David:

I am wearied from groaning;

All night long my pillow is wet with tears;
I melt my couch with weeping.
Grief dims my eyes;
They are worn out with all my woes.
Away from me, all you evildoers,
For Hashem has heard the sound of my weeping.
Hashem has heard my entreaty;
Hashem will accept my prayer.
All my enemies will be confounded and dismayed;
They shall turn away in sudden confusion.
Oh Hashem, my God, in Thee I find refuge;
Save me, rescue me from my pursuers,
Before they tear at my throat like a lion,
and carry me off beyond hope of rescue.

He finally fell into a fitful sleep

The next morning broke blinding white, and it was evident that it would bring no reprieve from the storm. A smile crinkled the innkeeper's peasant face as he stomped into the chilly barn carrying a fresh vat of steaming kasha. "Come on, boys, this will warm your stomachs," he urged. The children devoured the kasha while the innkeeper looked on with satisfaction. He then winked broadly as he confided that the roads were impassable.

"You boys are in luck. Those two privates refused to leave here today, and they finally got that corporal to agree to stay on until the weather improves. Those fellows are just plain afraid that the horses will leave them stranded.

Besides, they have plenty of vodka. Nothing like vodka to convince a man to stay put in this kind of weather, heh?"

For three days the snowbound children stayed in the barn, and the charitable innkeeper did not permit them to starve. The brief respite restored some of their strength, but Yankeleh feared for their flagging spirits, so on the very first day of their stopover in Petrovaskoy he called upon every ounce of his own limited energy and started teaching again.

He began by reminding the children to daven Shacharis. After Shacharis he recounted *midrashim* praising the heroism of our forefathers and sages, and quoted from *Pirkei Avos*, drawn from memory, which he hoped would help them to remain firm in their faith. They ate an afternoon meal of bread softened in the milk they had learned to urge from the not-always-accommodating cows. Then Yankeleh had them all take an afternoon nap. Between Minchah and Maariv, he led them in singing *nigunim*. In soft voices, weakened by starvation and suffering, they sang praises to the Almighty. Yankeleh looked into their trusting eyes, his heart aching. Before settling into sleep, he went from boy to boy, giving each one individual words of encouragement. Only then would he allow himself to rest.

"You are amazing, Yankeleh," Reuven muttered, shaking his head, "Don't you ever get tired?"

Yankeleh looked into his friend's weary eyes. "It is I who am always amazed at you, Reuven. You stand by my side, never questioning, keeping pace with me, answering my call, comforting the children, ready to do battle with our enemies. For me it is a simple matter. I have a mission to fulfill as the son of the Kronitzer Rebbe. But what gives you the strength to stand by me?"

Reuven rubbed his chin. "I guess I have become one of your Chassidim," he grinned. "And whatever my rebbe requires of me, I will do."

Yankeleh chuckled. "I am proud to have you as a Chassid."

As morning broke on the second day in Petrovaskoy, the freezing winds blew even stronger. The children remained huddled together in the barn, their bodies numb from the cold. When the barn door flew open and the smiling innkeeper lumbered in carrying a pot of soup, they let out a shout and rushed forward, almost knocking the poor man over. He ladled out watery soup with an occasional potato and soggy green onion bobbing on its surface, but no one complained. It was more than they could have hoped for. Leibeleh Bronfman stared down into his bowl and sighed. "I can still taste my mother's chicken soup with the egg noodles floating in it," he said, licking his lips at the memory.

"Just give me my mother's chopped onions and liver and the chicken fat *gribbenes*," Hershel Hochstein called out. "And my mother's sweet kugel with raisins and honey, and the tzimmes." His eyes closed as he savored the memory.

"What was your favorite?" eleven-year-old Mendeleh Feinberg called out to Yankeleh.

Yankeleh cocked his head to the side, closing his eyes for a second. "Hmm," he said, as he recalled the huge platter of gefilte fish that his mother set on the table every Friday night.

"Give me the head and tail of the carp," he muttered, almost to himself. "And on holidays there was a goose roasted crisp and delicious."

"We were poor," Reuven admitted, "but poor or not, on Shabbos my mother's cholent was the best. There was always a stuffed neck and a kugel right in the pot. It came out brown and delicious, and the beans and potatoes were dark brown and peppery, and the pieces of meat were thick and juicy."

The talk of food and home somehow eased their gnawing hunger and comforted them. That day and the next, they learned Torah and rested. By the time they had to leave Petrovaskoy their faces were less drawn and their eyes were brighter. As they stepped out into a world cloaked in white and adorned with rainbows of glistening icicles, they gasped with delight. The dry snow crackled and crunched beneath their feet and the crisp fresh air was invigorating.

But the long trek to Rostov was exhausting. By the time they arrived at the army base, it was already dark. Their legs were wobbling, their bodies numb from the cold.

Corporal Yusopovich saluted the lieutenant who came forward to meet them. "These are the conscripts from Nikolayev, sir," he said, flicking a sidelong glance at the motley group. He handed his orders to the officer.

"At ease, Corporal," the lieutenant commanded. He stared in revulsion at the conscripts. "Why do they look so poor, Corporal?"

"You know how it is, sir. These are mollycoddled yids," he grunted. "What can you expect?"

"It says here that you were to deliver sixteen conscripts. I count only thirteen, corporal."

"The others died on the way, sir," he replied with an indifferent shrug.

"You are dismissed, Corporal," the lieutenant barked, eyeing him coldly. "Private Petrov, show these men to their quarters."

He glanced once again at the children, his jaw tightening. Before turning on his heel, he bellowed, "And take these children to their quarters, too."

Minutes later, the boys staggered into a huge room with cots lined up in two neat rows. No sooner had they crossed the threshold than they were met by a fleshy faced sergeant who pointed to a sack in the middle of the room and told the conscripts to throw their filthy rags into it. They were then led into an adjoining bathhouse and ordered to climb into a huge vat and scrub themselves with harsh, thick bristle brushes. They climbed out of the tubs to find themselves besieged by a crew of scowling barbers, who, without a word, shaved off tangles of lice-infested hair. Back in the barracks, they pulled on the adult-size shirts and pants, which hung on their starved bodies like so many burlap bags. The sergeant, who introduced himself as Gregor Tiomkin, handed them rope to keep their pants up. And so attired, they trudged to the mess hall, where trays of steaming food awaited them. The children stared at one another in disbelief, and for a brief moment they were in paradise.

But one day of paradise was not enough to erase the scars of months of starvation. That night Yankeleh was once again awakened by the sounds that separated life from death. In hushed tones he called to Reuven. The two friends found Mendeleh Feinberg gasping for air. They stared at one another, frantic, not knowing how to help Mendeleh in his desperate struggle for life. Leaving Reuven at Mendeleh's side, Yankeleh rushed off in search of help. An angry and bleary-eyed Sergeant Tiomkin mumbled curses as he followed Yankeleh back to the barracks, but it was too late. There was nothing left to do. The sergeant wrapped the child's body in a blanket and shuffled out without a word.

By morning, rumors about the cause of Mendeleh's death had spread panic throughout the camp: the Jewish conscripts carried the plague. Violence filled the air. Sullen soldiers banded together, their eyes burning with fear and hate.

"Let's kill the yids, before they kill us," they shouted as they swarmed toward the children's barracks. It was clear to both the lieutenant and the sergeant that they would soon have a massacre on their hands, and neither had the stomach for a pogrom in the well-ordered and tightly disciplined Rostov barracks. Whether they liked it or not, they had to defuse the volatile situation.

Sergeant Tiomkin stepped in front of the advancing mob. "No one goes near the conscripts' barracks. They are in quarantine, and they will stay in quarantine until we are sure that no one else is sick. Just remember, you ignorant louts, these conscripts are the responsibility of the Rostov Army Command, under the direct jurisdiction of His Majesty, the Czar. Not one of those boys is to be touched. Is that understood? Not one! Now cool your tempers and get back to your barracks. Is that clear? You tangle with me and you face court-martial," he barked.

The sergeant's words were greeted with angry murmurs, but after some hesitation the men disbanded. By mid-afternoon it appeared that all had been forgotten, at least so the sergeant and lieutenant hoped. Fortunately for the children, they were unaware of the uproar outside, or how very close they had come to being harmed.

For the moment all the boys could think about was the death of their friend Mendeleh. For the first time since they had left Nikolayev they wept openly and voiced their fears. Velvel Breitbart spoke for all of them, revealing what they had in their hearts. He wailed that death stalked them and that the future was hopeless. "We'll never survive the winter," he cried out bitterly, rubbing the tears from his reddened eyes. "We are doomed, all of us. If we don't die now, we'll die in a month from now, or a year. It's no use going on, fighting for what, for what kind of life, for what kind of future?"

"No, no, you mustn't talk like that, Velvel. We mustn't give up," Reuven pleaded with him. "That's what they want us to do. Don't you see, Velvel? They want us to turn away from our faith, to become *goyim*, and they will do everything possible to wear us down, to make us feel that there is no hope unless we become traitors to our own people. We have come through so much together, and look at us, we're alive, we're still here. And that is the worst thing we can do to them—to survive as Jews." He extended his hands imploringly. "I know it's hard, but if you give up and join them, what have you done? You have joined the haters, the murderers of Jewish children. Is that what you want? Is that who you want to be?"

Velvel bit his lip, still sniffling as he shook his head no.

"Then we will stick together. We will become better Jews, and we will survive. That, Velvel, is our hope, our only hope."

Yankeleh felt that his heart would burst with emotion as he listened to Reuven. He had been ready to intervene, to offer words of encouragement, but now he just sat back and listened, his palms pressed to his forehead. His dear friend Reuven had said it all.

Yankeleh considered Velvel's words and felt as if a knife had been jabbed in his ribs, for he saw clearly how suffering had planted the seeds of despair in the hearts of the younger children. He had to find a way to give them hope, to bring them closer to Torah. Time was growing short. It was only a matter of months before they would be separated, and who knew what the future held for them. He had heard rumors that some of them would be sent to work for peasants until their eighteenth birthday, when they would be inducted into the army. Others were to be dispatched to distant army bases in the north. And as always, the baptismal font loomed before them—like a terrible sword hanging over their heads. He shuddered. "What will happen to my young friends?" he thought. "Who will be there to teach them, to keep them close to their faith? Without Torah they will be lost."

Another thought plagued him. He wanted with

all of his heart for little Mendeleh to have a Jewish burial. But how? He decided that no matter what the consequences he had to speak to Sergeant Tiomkin. That afternoon, when the sergeant came to inspect the barracks, Yankeleh approached him, his heart pounding. With head bowed and eyes lowered, he spoke. "Sir," he began, "sir, is it possible…that is, could Mendel Feinberg be given a Jewish burial?"

The astonished sergeant stared in amazement at Yankeleh. He shrugged his shoulders. "I don't know," he said, shaking his head. "We usually bury soldiers in the military cemetery or send the bodies home for burial. Wasn't the boy baptized?"

"We are all Jews, Sergeant," Yankeleh stated firmly, his eyes meeting the gaze of the sergeant.

The sergeant scratched his head. "I'll speak to Lieutenant Suslovsky. Maybe we can get one of your… your priests to bury the boy."

Yankeleh looked away, unable to hide the tears rolling down his cheeks. "Thank you," he said hoarsely, "thank you."

The sergeant headed toward the lieutenant's quarters, shaking his head in wonder. He had planned to speak to Lieutenant Alexei Suslovsky about the conscripts, and now with this strange request, well, what better time than the present? The sergeant was no Jew-lover, but thinking about the wretched condition of the conscripts still made him angry. There were limits. He knew that the lieutenant had been equally shocked by the sight of the children. The orders had called for the conscripts to be marched north to Perm, but Lieutenant Suslovsky had countermanded the orders, reporting back that the conscripts were in no physical condition to undertake so difficult a march. He had told the sergeant that he would put the boys to work in the camp. There was plenty to do, particularly the dirty chores that the men griped about, he had said.

When the sergeant passed on Yankeleh's request to Lieutenant Suslovsky, the lieutenant threw his hands in the air. "Get in touch with the *kahal* in Rostov; they'll take care of it," he declared indifferently. "It makes no difference to me, one way or the other," he said. "Let them bury their own."

He then uncharacteristically ordered the sergeant to treat the boys decently. "When the lads are stronger and we lift that stupid quarantine, I leave the work schedule in your hands."

Before the month was out, a roster was hung in the barracks. The boys were ordered to clean the latrines, keep the horses' stalls clean and dry, brush down the horses, and polish the boots of the officers, in addition to the duties in the kitchen, which would have made any other recruit grit his teeth with disgust. But for the boys, nothing was too demeaning after the nine months of terror and misery they had endured. At least in the army camp in Rostov no one paid much attention to them as long as they did not complain and completed their chores. But Yankeleh knew that this was merely a way station and that the peace of Rostov was an illusion. He worried about the children, whom he had grown to love as brothers. He was determined more than ever to continue their nightly lessons with even greater diligence.

Night after night, Yankeleh's frail body rocked to and fro, his eyes aflame.

"What does the Torah mean to us, my friends? What does it mean to be a Jew?" he would begin his lesson. "Children, when you think of the Torah, I want you to think of it as water, for Torah purifies and cleanses us from all that is debasing in life. Torah, my friends, is our manna: it sustains us at all times and is there for all, for rich and for poor alike. And our Torah is as sweet as honey because it frees us from bitterness and from hatred. Try to remember that our Torah is our crown, for it sets us above all God's creatures."

The children sat in awed silence, their eyes reflecting their wonder. As he looked into their faces, Yankeleh prayed with all of his heart that his little friends would remember and keep the commandments.

He leaned over and patted Avrumaleh's hand. "Now children, do you know that God had decided to give everlasting life to the nation that would accept the Torah? And when Israel accepted the Torah they gained supremacy over the Angel of Death!"

The children gasped. "And what happened?" Pesach Simchah Bass asked, his eyes shining with curiosity.

"What happened?" he intoned, shaking his head sadly. "The children of Israel forgot their promise to God and they worshipped the Golden Calf. And as a punishment for this, their sin, God said they would have to study the Torah in suffering and bondage, in exile and unrest, amid cares of life and burdens, until, in the Messianic times and in the future world, God would compensate them for all of their sufferings. But, my friends, until that time there is no sorrow that falls to Israel's lot that is not in part a punishment for their worship of the Golden Calf."

"We will be faithful to the Torah. We won't disappoint the Holy One, blessed be His name," Pesach Simchah cried out.

Yankeleh stared at the children. Then he bid them all sleep well.

"Tomorrow is another day, a day for learning," he promised with a wan smile.

With the breath of spring came mud—thick, viscous mud that clung like glue. It seemed to the conscripts that all they did day and night was polish the boots of their officers, struggling in vain against the ubiquitous mud. Yankeleh had been assigned to care for the horses and to clean their stalls, and much to his surprise, he discovered that this was one chore that he did not mind. In fact he enjoyed the work. Physical activity eased his torment. Scrubbing down the stallions, he would smile with satisfaction as they nuzzled him in appreciation. He would confide in them, and share with them his agonizing fears.

He had just brushed down a whinnying mare, and was about to continue his rounds, when Hershel Hochstein's voice startled him out of his reverie.

"Yaakov," he shouted, "the sergeant's looking for you."

Yankeleh dropped the brush. His heart pounding, he rushed back toward the barracks.

FIVE

I DON'T KNOW what's worse, wolves in winter or mosquitoes in summer," Private Ivan Yurovsky muttered half to himself, his eyes narrowing as he flicked the horses' reins. Yankeleh sat next to Yurovsky while Private Yusup Sivobluy snored loudly in the back of the wagon. The two privates had been reassigned to Kirov and were ordered to escort the conscript to their new base. Yankeleh listened to Yurovsky's complaints with half an ear as he swatted the mosquitoes, stimulated to a frenzy by the warm, humid weather. They had been on the road, heading north, for over two weeks, with at least another two weeks to go before they would reach their destination.

Yankeleh had known from the very first day in Rostov that their stay there was only temporary. Still, when the orders came, he felt a cold fear grip his heart. Sergeant Tiomkin never looked up at the boys as he gripped the sheaf of papers in his hand and cleared his throat. "Some of you lads are shipping out. Up north to Serov," he announced. "But the boys under twelve will be staying here for the time being."

Yankeleh noticed the sergeant masking his emerging smile with a scowl. All the boys were grateful to the sergeant, who, for some unfathomable reason, had shown them kindness and seemed to have even grown fond of them. It was obvious that he was reluctant to see them leave.

The sergeant peered down his list and began rattling off the familiar names. "Hershel Hochstein, Reuven Fenster, Simchah Wachsman. You boys will be heading north for Serov in the morning," he called out. "This time in a wagon."

Everyone laughed nervously, but Yankeleh stared straight ahead. The sergeant never looked his way, and his expression remained veiled. "Yaakov Halevi will leave for Kirov the following day."

Gripped by a strange premonition, Yankeleh shuddered. "Why can't I go with the others?" he asked.

"Those are the orders," the sergeant snapped as he stalked out.

The boys gathered about Yankeleh, trying to fathom the reason for his being separated from the rest of the conscripts. Yankeleh was certain that it had not been an arbitrary decision. His superiors saw him as having too much influence over the boys: It was clear to everyone that the children idolized him. And now they were separating him from the boys in order to speed up the process of their conversion to good Christian soldiers.

The memory of parting from Reuven still tormented him. There was nothing they could do but promise one another to remain loyal Jews and friends forever.

"I am your Chassid, remember?" Reuven had said, embracing his friend. "One day, Yankeleh, one day, God willing, we will be together in Kronitz Podolsk, and I will sit at your table and learn."

Yankeleh was jolted from his reverie by the cart lurching and careening to the right, startling the sleeping private in the wagon. The horses reared and the wagon came to a shivering halt. Yankeleh and Private Yurovsky were thrown from their perch. Stumbling to their feet they brushed the dust off their clothes.

"Hey, what's going on?" Sivobluy yelled as he scrambled from the wagon.

"What d'ya think's going on, you idiot?"

The soldiers surveyed the cart's damaged wheel. They shook their heads morosely, defeated before they started.

"We ain't got tools, nothing," Yurovsky muttered, glaring helplessly at the wheel that had all but fallen from its axle.

"Well, we got our shoulders, ain't we? We gotta lift the rotten wagon and fix the wheel or we ain't going no place," Sivobluy snorted.

"Who d'ya think you are, ordering me about, Private Sivobluy," Yurovsky sneered, poking his finger at the other man.

Before Yankeleh knew what was happening, the two were rolling on the ground, pounding each other with their fists. Yankeleh looked on, stone-faced. For all he cared they could stay there forever. These last two weeks were the first taste of freedom he had known in a year. He certainly wasn't in any hurry to get to Kirov. Luckily for him, the two peasant soldiers had been warned by Sergeant Tiomkin to protect the conscript at all costs. As long as they had enough money to buy vodka and black bread, they seemed content enough to ignore the boy, and the sergeant's orders served to protect Yankeleh from their constant brawling.

The men struggled to their feet, shouting curses at each other. "Aw, come on, we gotta fix the wagon."

It was decided that Sivobluy would remove the wheel and repair it. But the wagon had to be lifted, and Yurovsky eyed Yankeleh with undisguised distaste.

"Hey, yid, get your hands out of your pockets and help." Given no other choice, Yankeleh rolled up his sleeves and took a deep breath. The two squatted and, with a groan, managed to lift the wagon long enough for Sivobluy to remove the wheel, repeating the feat again when the mended wheel was ready to be replaced.

Yankeleh wiped the perspiration from his brow with his sleeve, a smile on his lips.

"Not bad for a yid," Yurovsky sniggered. "You got some muscle in those skinny arms," he guffawed, smacking Yankeleh on the back in an unexpected show of camaraderie.

Once alone in the back of the wagon Yankeleh ran

his hand over his upper arm, amazed at the peach-sized muscle that emerged. Although the year of deprivation had left Yankeleh skin and bones, three months spent at the Rostov base had put some meat back on him. And now, though lean, he also had some muscle to show for the months of physical activity. The year had also added five inches to his height. At the age of fourteen he was now almost five feet eight inches tall. He leaned his head against the wagon and unconsciously rubbed his recently shaved head, but now his fingers found a growing crop of curls. He sighed, closed his eyes, and allowed the warm sun to lull him into much needed sleep.

The wagon rolled into the Kirov army base at dusk. It took little time for the two privates to be shown their quarters, leaving Yankeleh to the mercies of a gruff, tobacco-chewing corporal.

"So you're the yid from Rostov," he grunted, spitting out a wad of moist tobacco at Yankeleh's feet. The corporal grabbed Yankeleh by the scruff of his neck. He dragged him through the compound to a small, wooden shack and shoved him into a dank, closet-sized room. When Yankeleh's eyes adjusted to the gloom, he flinched at the sight of another boy.

"Welcome to Kirov," the lad drawled cynically. "My name is Yisroel Brodsky from the village of Kabaney in Kiev Gubernya."

They shook hands formally. Yankeleh stared at Yisroel Brodsky's face. Even in the dark of their prison, Yankeleh could discern the welts and bruises.

"You're wondering about these?" Yisroel inquired,

pointing to his mangled face.

Yankeleh swallowed hard and nodded yes.

"I guess the corporal just doesn't like me," he said with a resigned shrug. And then, bending closer to Yankeleh, he warned, "Just be careful of that monster."

"You mean he beat you for no reason?"

"I'm a Jew—isn't that enough reason?"

Yankeleh shivered. "How long have you been a conscript?" he asked.

"I was kidnapped last year, and they had me in some mud hole near Kiev with thirty others. The little ones all died," the boy replied, his voice taking on a hard edge, "and they beat their *goyishkeit* into the others."

"And you?"

"I'm tougher than I look," he grinned, "so they sent me up here. Haven't you heard? Kirov is the dumping ground for the special cases. You know, the older boys who have survived the softening-up process and haven't knuckled under. You get my meaning?" And then, pounding his brow with the palm of his hand, he exclaimed, "Hey, here I am talking about myself and I don't even know your name."

Yankeleh managed a weak smile and introduced himself.

Yisroel gasped. "*Ribono Shel Olam*! You're the son of the Kronitzer Rebbe!" The seemingly hardened conscript leaned over and patted Yankeleh's arm. "They won't get us. We'll leave here as Jews, dead or alive, right, Yaakov?"

Tears gathered in the corners of Yankeleh's eyes.

"Dead or alive, Yisroel."

In the middle of the night the door creaked open. Yankeleh started. In the pitch darkness he made out the stolid form of the corporal. He gasped when the butt of a rifle struck across Yisroel Brodsky's back. The boy jumped to his feet, drawing away from his attacker. The corporal grabbed him and, without uttering a word, shoved him forcefully from the room.

Yankeleh spent the rest of the night davening for his new friend. Finally, a sliver of sunshine flickering across his face told him that morning had arrived. Hours passed before the door opened again. To Yankeleh's relief, it was only a bow-legged private who poked his head in and shoved a bowl of gruel and some water into the cell. Yankeleh filled the long hours with davening and learning. As the sun's rays dipped lower, fading into dusk, Yisroel still had not returned.

The days passed uneventfully. There were no visitors, no change of routine, and no Yisroel. If not for the private bringing Yankeleh his daily ration of slop and some water, he would have imagined that they had forgotten all about him. But he soon found to his misfortune that this was not the case.

On the fourth day, it was the corporal himself who pushed open the door. Yankeleh jumped to his feet. Without a word, the corporal pinioned Yankeleh's arms behind him and dragged him into the blinding morning brightness. He kicked and pushed Yankeleh across the compound toward a distant barracks, finally flinging him into a small room. The corporal growled, "Here he is, all ready for you, Father Nicolai."

Father Nicolai pointed to a chair for Yankeleh to sit in. The rotund priest stood over him, examining the conscript curiously while stroking his scraggly beard. "So, my son, you are Yaakov Yitzchak Halevi from Kronitz Podolsk?" he said with a friendly pat on the back.

Yankeleh nodded.

The priest handed Yankeleh a glass of water. "Come, drink up. It's very warm today."

Quietly saying the *brachah*, Yankeleh gulped down the water, the first food or drink he had had that morning.

"So, young man, I am told that you are reluctant to join our ways," Father Nicolai said. "Perhaps you are not fully aware of the rewards ahead, not only in the afterlife, but in this life as well. Those who accept our savior are well cared for by the Church. Perhaps you may even find a career in our Church. A great opportunity presents itself before you, Yaakov Yitzchak," he said, raising his brow and nodding.

Yankeleh stiffened.

"I didn't hear your reply," Father Nicolai said sharply. "When a priest of the Holy Russian Church addresses you, he expects an answer."

Yankeleh looked into the eyes of the priest. He had seen the same burning fanaticism before, and he winced as the memory surfaced. "Sir, you must know that it isn't possible for me to accept your generous offer. I am a Jew and I intend to stay a Jew."

"Such a stubborn attitude from one so young," the priest sneered, his face darkening.

A terrible rage welled up within him, and Yankeleh could control his anger no longer. He cried out, "How can you ask me to join your church, the church that tears Jewish children from their mothers and murders them by the thousands? It is your church whose followers have slaughtered hundreds of thousands of my people over the centuries. And now you ask me to join you?"

The priest grew livid, and pounded the table with his fist. The corporal bounded in. "This boy needs some discipline. And don't spare the rod," he fumed.

Yankeleh was yanked from his seat and dragged into the courtyard. He was tied to a stake with bruising leather thongs. The corporal, wielding a cat-o'-nine-tails, tore mercilessly at his body, beating him again and again until he finally fainted. A bucket of water revived him and the punishment continued.

Somewhere in the twilight between agony and numbness, Yankeleh was untied and dragged back to face the priest. Brushing his lips against Yankeleh's ear, he muttered, "This is your penance for sinning against our savior. If you don't atone and admit the error of your ways, you will taste more of the cat tomorrow," he promised.

Yankeleh did not recall being taken back to his cell. Nor was his friend Reuven there to succor him and help ease the pain. That night he was besieged by a pantheon of demons, their distorted faces taunting him.

The sting of ice water drew him back to consciousness.

He tried to move, but each movement was agony. He felt on fire. The corporal pulled him to his feet, and he was once again dragged across the yard to be tied to the stake. The corporal held the whip under Yankeleh's nose, his grin sadistically menacing. "Your friend Yisroel Brodsky was wiser than you, yid. He has already accepted our Christian faith," he growled.

Yankeleh winced and shook his head no.

Suddenly the evil apparition of the black-robed priest edged toward him.

"Accept the cross and you will be saved from punishment," he bellowed.

Yankeleh shut his eyes. "No, no, no!" he screamed. "No!" Once again the whip ripped his raw back. The flogging did not stop until Yankeleh was unconscious.

* * *

He did not know how many days had passed. Nor could he recall being taken to the infirmary, delirious with fever, or having his wounds dressed. But now, as he regained consciousness, a brisk breeze brushed his face and he could smell autumn in the air. An orderly bent over and offered a sip of water. The room spun around him. He rubbed his eyes and the room slowly came into focus.

"You were very bad," the orderly said gruffly. "Never thought you guys would make it."

Yankeleh turned his head away, blinking against the stinging sunlight. "Where am I? What happened to me?" he asked, dazed.

The orderly replied. "You and the other kid were brought to the army infirmary in pretty bad shape. Everybody thought you were both goners."

Yankeleh turned his head. There was another bed just a few feet away. Was he seeing things?

"Yisroel?" he cried out, his voice hoarse. "Yisroel?"

The other boy, his face chalk-white, blinked his eyes open. He gasped. "Yaakov? But they swore…they said that you had been baptized."

"They told me the same about you, Yisroel. But I never believed it, never once," Yankeleh whispered, his hand reaching out to grasp Yisroel's.

SIX

FOR REASONS NEVER made clear to them, the boys were kept in the infirmary long after their wounds had healed, and all that remained were ugly crimson scars as momentos. They spent their time talking and learning, and over the weeks their friendship blossomed. Yankeleh came to learn a great deal about his new friend. Srulik may have been tough and brave, but homesickness bore through his soul, compelling him to talk about Kabaney, his family, and his father in particular.

"My father was a cobbler," he said, almost apologetically. "As a child I used to stand near him as he would cut a piece of leather. I watched as he took its shapeless form and made it into a shoe. It just amazed me, and I thought my father was a genius, a real artist. I loved the smell of the leather—it had a rich aroma that drew me to my father's workroom. I couldn't wait to start helping him. I must have been very young, maybe three or four, when he took me on his knee and let me polish a small piece of leather. Much later he allowed me to use his precious knives to cut the leather. I remember how he held my hand, warning me to be very careful, since the leather was costly. It seemed funny to me at the time—imagine worrying about the leather and not about my hand! I still remember feeling like a king when my father complimented me and said that I would someday become a true craftsman. The truth is I am a pretty good cobbler," he added with a broad smile that held more than a touch of pride.

After a while Yankeleh detected that beneath Srulik's gruff and easygoing ways, there was exceptional intelligence. He was ignorant and unlearned in many ways, but he listened eagerly as Yankeleh taught him words of Chumash and *halacha*, retaining all he heard in his excellent memory. Their daily lessons became a source of joy and delight to both teacher and student.

"You know," Srulik said one day, his voice wistful, "my cheder rebbe, Reb Chuna, once appealed to my father to send me off to yeshiva for further study. I overheard him tell my father that I was a clever lad and that I should have the chance to learn." He shrugged his shoulders, his eyes clouding over. "But we were so poor. My father needed me to work with him to keep us from starving. I guess he just needed another pair of hands," he said philosophically.

Surprisingly, adversity had not drained away Srulik's sense of humor. With a wink, he often teased Yankeleh. "Maybe I, too, am an *ilui,* Yankeleh. But I ask you, who would take notice of a cobbler-*ilui*?" Other times he would turn solemn, his eyes burning with an inner fury. "Yankeleh, the curse of the poor is that their children are tied to ignorance by their poverty."

In a moment of candor, he revealed to Yankeleh that the village rabbi had actually offered to give his father the money for Srulik to attend yeshiva. "Imagine the rabbi coming to our poor home to plead with my father for me. He tried to assure my father that even poor boys manage to survive in the yeshiva. He reminded him that there were always Jewish homes where the yeshiva boys could *ess taig*, you know, where the boys could get a free daily meal. I know that he was disappointed when my father refused. I wanted to scream, to tell my father that he was denying me my chance to escape the ignorance of poverty. Why was he doing this to me? I had sleepless nights thinking about it.

"But now that I look back I don't feel any bitterness toward him anymore, just sorrow. I understand his dilemma. What could he do? We lived in a poor village, and *parnasah* was hard to come by. And without me... Believe me, Yankeleh, my father was not an unfeeling man, but with five daughters and just one son, well, who else was there to work at his side?"

The words stung Yankeleh. When he looked into Srulik's eyes, he knew the pain that his friend felt. He threw his arm about Srulik's shoulders.

"Srulik, when we get out of this, I want you to come to Kronitz Podolsk. There, with God's help, we will learn together properly."

"You are a good fellow, Yankeleh," Srulik replied, "but God only knows if we will ever escape. We are prisoners, even if we are not surrounded by prison walls. Do you know that they watch us all the time? And when we're eighteen, if we live so long, then off we go to serve the Czar for twenty-five years. By the time we meet again, we'll be too old for anything but the grave."

Yankeleh shook his head. "We can't give up, Srulik. We have to hold fast not only to our faith, but to hope. Czars don't live forever," he said with an encouraging smile. "Srulik, I'm no *navi*, but I feel in my bones that somehow, some way, we'll survive all of this."

On a day when the clouds hung low and dark, Yankeleh and Srulik left Kirov. As the rickety wagon clattered off, they both spat in the direction of the camp, as if on cue. They burst out laughing, pounding on each other's backs. They had both expressed their deepest feelings about the army base.

The cart jostled into a village some thirty miles from Kirov. The sergeant handling the wagon motioned to Srulik to get off. The boys clasped hands, both forcing brave smiles. No words were exchanged.

Yankeleh watched with trepidation as the sergeant shoved Srulik into a thatched cottage, returning minutes later with a vicious grin pasted on his face. "Raising some pigs will do that little yid some good," he growled. He then flicked the reins vigorously and they were once again on the open road. As the miles lumbered by, Yankeleh whiled the time away looking at the peasants gathering in the last yields of their harvest. The scent of alfalfa was still in the air. Yankeleh tried to enjoy the beautiful scene, avoiding as much as possible thoughts of his destination.

It was dusk before they clattered into the outskirts of Volodga. A florid-faced peasant trudged out from the cottage toward them, his boots muddied, his eyes vodka-sheathed.

"The boy looks too skinny," he muttered.

"What do you expect, a Jew with muscles? He'll get his muscles here," the sergeant cackled, throwing the bundle of Yankeleh's belongings to the ground.

Yankeleh jumped from the wagon, standing with his head bowed before his new master.

The peasant grunted. "Ever work on a farm?"

Yankeleh shook his head no.

"Got something for a thirsty soldier?" the sergeant asked the peasant, who stood frowning.

For the moment Yankeleh was forgotten as the two men took deep swigs from a bottle of vodka. Yankeleh surveyed the farm. The house was typical, a one-room, thatched cottage in which the entire family lived, often with their chickens, goats, and an army of other livestock that happened to be in the neighborhood. A troop of clucking chickens were now being shooed out of the cottage by a drawn, work-worn woman, no doubt the peasant's wife. The stench of animal dung hung everywhere, and the yard swarmed with flies. Goats munched on whatever they found, and geese and ducks waddled by like so many old matrons. On the side of the barn several fat pigs wallowed in the mud. Two horses, tied to a wooden stake, swished their tails rhythmically in an effort to rid themselves of the flies and mosquitoes clustering on their backs. One look at his new master and Yankeleh knew that he was one of the millions of Russian peasants who worked as tenant farmers for the wealthy nobles. The spoils of their back breaking toil were taken from them as payment for living in abject poverty.

Though not surrounded by armed guards and metal gates, he knew there was no chance of escape. Hundreds of bitter miles, thousands of unfriendly peasants, and the great army of the Czar lay between this thatched hut and the warm comfort of his parents' village. Yankeleh took a deep breath. This was now home.

Before leaving, the sergeant cackled, "Remember, Vlad Stepanovich Ruszky, turn this one into a good Russian Christian."

The peasant replied with an apathetic wave of the hand.

Yankeleh was relieved when the brutish peasant grunted that he was to sleep in the barn.

That night, sprawled across the sweet-smelling hay, Yankeleh gazed at the cows nearby, listening to the grinding sound as they chewed their cud. The barn was warm, though an occasional gust of wind whistling through the slats warned of the approaching winter. Yankeleh drew the tattered quilt closer about him and tried to sleep, but sleep eluded him. His mind kept drawing him back to treasured childhood scenes. He tried to deepen the time-faded images of his parents, to see them clearly in his mind's eye. There they were, full of joy and life, their love and strength forever nurturing.

Yankeleh was awakened at dawn by the rooster's crow. He rubbed his sleep-heavy eyes and stumbled out of the barn to find himself face to face with his master, whose own eyes were still clouded with vodka. Without uttering a word, Vlad Stepanovich kicked Yankeleh hard in the ankles. Yankeleh drew away, and then dashed toward the cistern to escape the next clout.

He pulled off his shirt and took a deep breath before plunging his head into the freezing water. Shivering from the cold, he patted himself dry with his shirt. A strange prickle in his spine made him whirl about. A few feet away stood the peasant's family with expressions of shock on their faces. For a second, Yankeleh stared back in confusion, and then he understood—they were staring at his scarred back. Vlad Stepanovich Ruszky also stood by, scratching his tangled thatch of beard, he mouth agape. "Who did that to you, boy?"

Yankeleh bit his lip. "Your mother church," he blurted out.

"Holy mother of God," the peasant's wife cried out, "the priests did that to you?"

"Woman, stop sniveling or you'll get the same on your back. Now get on with the chores," the peasant snapped, with more bark than bite. Yankeleh pulled on his shirt, his face burning red. The family sauntered off without a further word or glance his way.

With winter closing in, Vlad Stepanovich lost little time in putting Yankeleh to work. For the first few days, Yankeleh did his best to keep his distance from the loutish peasant, remembering the kick he'd received on his first day on the farm. Much to Yankeleh's relief, however, after that first day his new master no longer attempted to strike him. Instead, he confined himself to cursing Yankeleh for his ineptness, kicking a bucket and stomping about screaming obscenities until his anger abated. The peasant's three sons were not so fortunate. Whenever Vlad was in a foul mood, he would take the whip to the hapless lads.

The beet and potato crops had to be harvested before winter set in, and there could be no slackers. Everyone worked feverishly. Only when winter embraced them did the pace grow less frantic, although there was still plenty to be done. Yankeleh was kept busy mending fences and the barn roof as well as preparing fodder for the livestock.

Yankeleh was only too happy to eat his evening meal alone in the barn. But as the days grew shorter and the snow piled higher, the peasant's wife, Katia Ivanova, insisted that Yankeleh take his evening meal with the family. In the close confines of the crowded cottage, Yankeleh came to know the Ruszky family more intimately.

The peasant's wife he surmised to be no older than his own mother, yet she was already bent in body and spirit, her eyes always filled with sorrow. Her infrequent smiles were reserved for her eldest daughter, Marina. The boys, Igor, Yuri, and Volya, ranging in age from six to ten, were mischievous lads, although the burdens of survival had marked them as well. Yankeleh gazed at them sympathetically and wondered if they had ever had the chance to be children. There were two daughters,

Stashia, about twelve, and Marina, who he guessed to be closer to his own age. Stashia was a typical Russian peasant girl, with a round, rosy, high-cheekboned face and long, unkempt, blond braids. Marina, on the other hand, seemed unlike the other children. Her hair, which she wore plaited neatly around her head, was thick and brown, and dark, compassionate eyes gazed out of her pale, sensitive face.

Yankeleh could not help wondering about her. Not only did Marina look different from the rest of the family, but her demeanor remained refined despite her coarse upbringing and surroundings. She was a modest, gentle girl, whose kindness was apparent in the manner in which she served her father, the way she assisted her mother, and even in the gentle tone she used with her sister and brothers, who frequently provoked her. She never raised her voice or used harsh language. When she served Yankeleh his supper, she averted her eyes, and always inquired about his health and whether he had enough to eat. Considering his status in the household, Yankeleh could not fail to be touched by her show of concern.

There were other things that puzzled him about this peasant family. When sodden with alcohol, which was frequent during the cold winter months, it took little to provoke Vlad to beat his wife and children. Yet though he might rant and rave, he never struck his eldest daughter. In fact, Yankeleh noticed that his tone with her was unusually tender.

On Christmas day, Katia Ivanova bundled the children off to church. On her return home, she served a meal that was just a bit more festive than usual. Otherwise, Christmas was no different from any other day in their impoverished household. But when Vlad Stepanovich handed his daughter Marina a decorative comb as a gift, Yankeleh stared in open astonishment. She kissed his grizzled cheek, and he, in turn, patted her head and planted a kiss on her forehead, a sign of paternal affection that Yankeleh had never seen him shower on his other children.

But it was another incident that truly confounded Yankeleh and troubled him for months. Just after the dinner meal, as Yankeleh prepared to bid the family goodnight, Katia Ivanova reminded her son Igor to go with Yankeleh and check whether the animals were secure for the night. As children do, Igor balked, whining that he did not want to leave the warmth of the house for the bitter cold outside.

Yankeleh smiled reassuringly, patting Igor's head. "It's all right, Katia Ivanova. Igor can stay indoors. I'll check the animals."

Katia Ivanova shook her head no. "Igor has his chores," she bristled, shaking a plump finger at her sulking son.

Turning toward Igor, Yankeleh shrugged his shoulders. "Come on, Igor, we'll race to the barn. It isn't all that terrible outside."

Igor scowled and mumbled under his breath, "You dirty Jew, mind your own business."

Yankeleh shrugged indifferently, but Vlad Stepanovich leaned over and struck his son sharply across the face. "You idiot," he said between clenched teeth. "Never speak that way to Yaakov, or to anyone, do you hear?" And then, pulling his son's ear painfully, he instructed, "We're all God's children, Jew and gentile. Now apologize to Yaakov."

A fuming Igor muttered an apology, and Yankeleh murmured his gratitude to the peasant. With his arms clutched about himself against the icy wind, Yankeleh trudged toward the barn with Igor at his side.

That night and many nights to follow he thought about the incident and wondered about Vlad Stepanovich's strange behavior. For some reason, the scene disturbed him. Why would Vlad Stepanovich strike his son for uttering a term that was almost second nature to a Russian? And "dirty Jew" was the least of the insults Jews had to endure. No matter how he tried to analyze the scene, he still could not make sense of it. True, Vlad Stepanovich never attended church, nor did he ever have a good word to say about the clergy. But Yankeleh was aware that Jew-baiting often had little to do with religious belief. It seemed that hating and killing Jews was almost second nature to the Russian people, something rooted deeply in their souls. No, there had to be another reason why a Russian peasant such as Vlad would defend a Jew. But what?

He thought about Katia Ivanova, who had always been kind to him though, unlike her husband, she was very devout. He had often seen her kneeling before the icon on the wall of the cottage. She would light a candle and murmur a prayer, mopping away the tears that crept down her creviced cheeks.

Other things about the family also struck him as unusual. He remembered with a shudder how the sergeant had reminded Vlad Stepanovich to turn him into a good Russian Christian, yet in all of the time he had been with the Ruszky family, religion had never been discussed. And one day, he explained to Katia Ivanova why he never ate meat, not really expecting her to understand. On the very next day she prepared a platter for him piled high with potatoes, beets and cabbage, much more than should have been his normal share. Even more astounding, several weeks later she revealed that she had managed to put aside a few kopeks and had purchased a new pot, which she said she would use just for his vegetables. Yankeleh was speechless. He knew only too well that for the Ruszky family such a purchase was a luxury.

"It is a small payment for your hard work," she proclaimed with a warm smile.

As the months slipped by, Yankeleh gave up trying to solve the mystery. Soon the incidents and his curiosity faded, meshing in with his daily life on the farm.

When not exhausted from his chores, Yankeleh would stroll off to the distant woods, where alone, he would inhale the spicy aroma of pine and savor his moment of solitude. In these rare moments he felt his soul refreshed. Coming upon a crocus, spring's first flower, Yankeleh would bend down to caress its pale, delicate petals, the thought of spring uplifting him.

One night he ventured out despite the brisk breeze, hoping to taste the sweetness of spring, though his breath still came out in vapors. As he gazed up in wonder at the clusters of stars and the sliver of the new moon he praised the Almighty for creating so beautiful a world. Lost in thought, Yankeleh failed to hear Katia Ivanova approaching. When she greeted him, he started.

"It is a pleasant night, isn't it?" she said softly, drawing her shawl about her shoulders. "You know, this is always my favorite time of year, a time when the earth is reborn," she said with a faint smile. And then her conversation took an unexpected turn. "I know that life has not been kind to you, Yaakov. To be taken from your home as a child, never to see your parents again, and to be treated so…so cruelly," she said, shaking her head sadly. "Czar Nicholas is a terrible, unfeeling man," she blurted out. "After all, aren't we all God's children?" she added plaintively, repeating the words her husband had used that night in rebuking his son.

"Yes," Yankeleh replied with a touch of cynicism. But then, moved by her kind words, he added, "I want to tell you how much I appreciate your being so generous to me. And especially your thoughtfulness about my food. You seem to understand something about our dietary laws."

Katia Ivanova grew wistful. "Many years ago," she began with a deep sigh, "I worked as a servant for a Jewish family in a town not too far from here. There weren't many Jews there—a few Jewish artisans, a rabbi, and a teacher. I worked for the teacher, the *melamed* as he was called. They were such good people, such good people," she repeated in a low and earnest voice.

"My Vlad also worked for them. You know he is very good with his hands, and he did lots of odd jobs for the other Jews in the town, too. We were both treated well. You know, Vlad is not really a bad man, but his lot has not been easy. He was an orphan and his childhood in the orphanage was one long hell," she intoned bitterly. "When he was eighteen he left the orphanage and began working at anything that he could find. When we married, we hoped that he would learn a trade. He wanted to become a blacksmith. But without money, no one would take him on as an apprentice. Only the Jews were good to Vlad. They gave him work, and if there had not been that terrible tragedy, who knows? Maybe in time we would have had enough money to pay for an apprenticeship."

She shivered, drawing the shawl even closer about her. "That was a terrible time…a terrible time. There was a pogrom and many innocent people were killed, including the *melamed*, his sweet wife, and…and their child." She paused for a moment, then continued. "When I heard about the pogrom, I rushed to their home. I hoped that maybe I could help them in some way, but I was too late. All I found was death. Everything was destroyed, boards ripped out, windows broken. The bandits were looking for gold. Imagine looking for gold from those poor people! Such fools," she cried, "such fools. The only gold the *melamed* had were his holy books. I have never in my life seen so many books. But they destroyed that gold. Every book was burned to ashes.

"But, Yaakov, they missed one book, a family Bible. I would have returned it to the rabbi, but he, too, was… was murdered. No one was left…not one," she said quietly. "I hope God forgave me for taking their Bible. I wanted something to remember them by, even though I can't read. Still I cherish that Bible more than anything I have. But now that I know you, Yaakov, I think the family would want you to have their Bible."

Yankeleh's eyes widened in astonishment. His voice catching with emotion, he muttered, "I would be very proud to have their Bible."

Katia Ivanova reached deep into the pocket of her apron, pulled out a small, leather-bound *Tanach* and handed it to Yankeleh. His hands trembling, he clasped it to his lips.

Yankeleh could not wait to get back to the barn. Once alone, his eyes straining in the dim light of the oil lamp, he opened the *Tanach*. His pulse quickened as he stared down at the names inscribed in beautiful Hebrew script on the first page:

> *Pesach ben Gershon ben Aharon*
> *Brachah bas Eliahu ben Yisrael Nahum*
> *Child: Miriam.*
> *Date of birth: First day of Shavuos: 1827*

That night Yankeleh could not sleep.

With the first breath of spring, the back-breaking work of tilling the soil began. Winter's tranquility ended with the rush to prepare the soil for seeding. Then, as the frenzied season of seeding and planting ended and the weather became warmer, Yankeleh would often take the goats and cows to pasture, a task he looked forward to. As he trudged through the meadows, his eyes alert for predators, he found time to gather in the beauty about him, gazing at the fields blanketed with wildflowers, inhaling the sweet bouquet of summer.

On one particularly warm day, Yankeleh was happy to escape the summer heat beneath the protective branches of an ancient sycamore. When the sun bid him to daven Minchah, he rose and gazed up to the blue sky, imagining himself for a brief moment as Avraham Avinu. After reciting his afternoon prayers, he reclined beneath the tree and began his daily study of *Tanach*. Engrossed in the pages of the precious book, the only *sefer* he had owned since that long-ago day that he'd been kidnapped, the hours flew by. When he raised his eyes again, the sun's fiery rays were angled low. He yawned and stretched, limbering his stiffened muscles. Suddenly he became aware of the ominous silence all around him. Where was his flock? He jumped to his feet in panic. What if some had been devoured by wild beasts?

He raced about, searching for the straying cows and goats. At last the missing animals were finally found, and a grateful Yankeleh sank beneath the tree to catch his breath. He brushed away an irritating mosquito buzzing in his ear and heaved a deep sigh of relief, now keeping his eyes peeled on the grazing herds. Moments later, billows of dust and the sound of hoofbeats caught his attention. Yankeleh pulled himself to his feet lazily, shielding his eyes against the glare of the setting sun. He peered into the distance. A single rider approached. As he came into view, Yankeleh gasped.

SEVEN

HIS CASSOCK WHIPPING about his legs, the young priest dismounted. He was a powerfully built man with a wavy, blond beard that straggled unkempt from the wind and the pace of the gallop. His smile was broad, and his blue eyes reflected pleasure at this unexpected encounter with a young peasant boy.

He extended his hand in greeting to Yankeleh, who watched him warily.

"Hello there. Sorry if I startled you. I'm the new priest here, Father Peter Fyodorovich Kuskov." He added with a sigh, "It must have been a shock losing old Father Yusep after so many years, but life and death are not in our hands." And then a warm smile edged out the frown. "And who are you? I don't believe I've seen you at church," he chuckled as he shook a finger at Yankeleh in mock reproach.

Yankeleh's jaw tightened. He had taken the priest's

hand perfunctorily and had listened to his affable greetings with a deep stirring of fear and hatred. "My name is Yaakov Yitzchak Halevi," he replied icily.

"I see. Well," he drawled, "now I understand why you haven't been over to our church." His manner remained open and friendly. "You must be one of the cantonist boys serving in the area." And then rubbing his chin, he shook his head in amazement. "Dressed as you are, well, you look like a typical peasant lad. I never would have guessed."

Yankeleh stared at the ground.

"May I join you under the tree? The weather has been beastly hot, and I think my horse needs a chance to cool off. I am afraid that I drive the nag too hard. I enjoy a good gallop and sometimes forget that the old steed is not a racer," he observed with a chuckle.

The priest looked at the silent young man now seated at his side with growing curiosity. "I take it you have resisted our proselytizing efforts?" he said lightly. "I guess our priests haven't been able to convince you. Well," he said, patting Yankeleh's shoulder, "I am ready to help you see the light; at least that's what the letter I received from the local authorities insists I must do. So, if you'll be a good fellow and drop by once or twice a week, we can review some of the thornier theological questions. I assure you I am a pleasant teacher."

Yankeleh's eyes narrowed. And then in a spontaneous gesture of defiance, he pulled up his shirt and turned his whip-wealed back to the startled priest. "I've had enough lessons to last me more than one lifetime," he spat out, his eyes burning with anger.

The priest exhaled a shocked gasp. "I…I am sorry, truly sorry. You…why, you have been terribly abused in the name of our beliefs, and this grieves me more than words can say," he said sincerely. And then, his voice wavering, he changed the subject. "And how does your master treat you?"

"He's all right."

"Well, thank the Lord for small mercies," the priest murmured.

"You know, I am pretty new here, just over three months. This is my first parish and I need time to acquaint myself with the local people. I still haven't met all of the villagers. Whom do you work for?"

"Vlad Stepanovich Ruszky."

"Hmm, Ruszky. Ah yes, I know his wife. She comes to church often. Seems like a good woman. I take it that Vlad Stepanovich is not much of a church-goer," he said with a faint grin. "You know, peasants can be stand-offish with a young, new priest after having had their comfortable old man with them for over twenty-five years. Still, I'd like to meet him."

And then, thrashing about for another avenue of conversation, the priest turned to his present circumstances. "You know, I originally come from Odessa. It's so very far from home and family, I suppose I'm a bit homesick. It takes some time getting used to a new place, and a tiny village is really a change for me. But I really shouldn't complain. It is a first parish and a priest has to start somewhere. And compared to what you've been through," he said with a sympathetic sigh, "well, it breaks my heart to think of children being taken from their homes so very young." He then leaned his head against the tree and closed his eyes briefly, running his long fingers absentmindedly through his beard. "Look here, Yaakov, I don't want your master to get into any trouble on your account. And I'm sure you wouldn't want any trouble for him either. You see, Yaakov, he has been made responsible for your Christian...let's call it your Christian development. And as I see it, he has trouble with his own Christian development," he chuckled. "I surely wouldn't want the authorities down on his head. These peasants have enough to worry about. And of course they will send you elsewhere if they aren't satisfied with the way your master is preparing you for future army service," he affirmed. "You see, he is required to bring you to church, or at least to religious instruction."

Yankeleh stared straight ahead, his jaw tightening.

"There must be a way to avoid causing more difficulties."

The priest cupped his chin in his hands. After a moment's thought he looked up, glancing eagerly at the quiet boy sitting beside him.

"Now look here, maybe we can make some kind of an arrangement between us. You come over to the parish every Wednesday after sunset, and we'll just sit and talk. I swear to you by all that I hold holy that I will not in any way harm you."

A less than convinced Yankeleh stared back. "You are wasting your time, sir."

"I imagine that I am," the priest replied stiffly. "But the law requires that I, that we, study together. And so, I am afraid that you have very little choice. Besides, I feel certain that there is much that you can teach me, Yaakov Yitzchak," he added, a faint smile emerging. "You see, I have inherited some books from my predecessor, and I think you just might find them interesting."

"What kind of books?"

"Ah," the priest said, holding his index finger up. "So you are interested in books? Good. Father Yusep, who from all accounts didn't sound like much of a scholar to me, nonetheless had, in his rather meager library, a full set of your Talmud." And then rubbing his ear, he remarked candidly, "No doubt it was given to him by some villager who pillaged it from a Jewish home."

Yankeleh stiffened. Could it have been from the home of the *melamed*? he wondered, his heart aching at the thought.

"When you come to see me next Wednesday, we may find some time to study your Talmud together. Is that a fair exchange for a few lessons from me? I admit that I skimmed through a few pages, and though I studied some Aramaic at the seminary, my knowledge of the language is limited. Now I have a feeling that your Aramaic is better than mine. And so we could study the texts together. You see, Yaakov, we can learn from each other," he cajoled, his voice a syrupy invitation. He rose and dusted off his cassock.

Yankeleh stared at the priest suspiciously.

Mounting his horse the priest called out, "I'm

heading out to Vlad Stepanovich's to tell him about our arrangement. See you on Wednesday, Yaakov," he shouted cheerily.

As he rode off, Yankeleh's stomach knotted. Still, he admitted, the thought of actually holding a Talmud in his hands was an enticing one. There were, he knew, several halachic problems when it came to learning Talmud with a non-Jew, but there were lenient opinions that could be relied on, particularly in light of his precarious situation.

A scowling Vlad Stepanovich greeted Yankeleh on his return home with his well-grazed and contented flock. "The priest was here," he grunted, his eyes narrowing. "I hate their parasitic guts," he spat out. "Every one of them, parasites, living off the sweat of our brows." Then he added quietly, "I've got to let you go on Wednesday nights, you know."

Yankeleh nodded, his eyes avoiding those of Vlad Stepanovich. The peasant stepped forward and unexpectedly patted Yankeleh's sagging shoulder. "Don't worry, boy. I ain't letting you go alone. I'm coming with you. No one will lay a hand on you," he assured, his voice hoarse.

"Thank you," Yankeleh murmured, rushing to the cistern to hide the emerging tears.

Dinner that night was a somber affair. Vlad Stepanovich drank too much, and the family nervously observed his growing vodka-induced rage with trepidation. Yuri unwisely punched Igor, and Vlad Stepanovich flared. He grabbed the whip and went for the boys with blind fury, slicing at their bodies cruelly.

The prelate's unexpected visit had indeed touched a tender nerve. Yankeleh rose uneasily, readying to leave the tense group, when Vlad growled, "We'll get him, don't you worry. We'll get him."

Yankeleh shivered as he strode toward the barn. Something in Vlad Stepanovich's voice disturbed him. He wondered what the priest might have said to upset him so fiercely. In his heart Yankeleh feared his respite was coming to an end. Once again he was being pursued. More than anything in this world, Yankeleh longed for his father's guidance, for his intellectual and emotional support. Now he had no one, not even a good friend to whom he could pour out his heart. He often wondered about Reuven and Srulik, never forgetting their special friendships, friendships that had grown out of mutual suffering. What was happening to his old friends? he wondered. He bit his lip, his heart aching for them, and for himself. The future seemed gloomier than ever.

On Tuesday night, the night before his scheduled meeting with Father Peter Fyodorovich Kuskov, Yankeleh gazed down at the *Tanach*, as the flickering light of the oil lamp cast an eerie shadow across its page. Through tear-filled eyes he attempted to read a passage in *Devarim*. And then, despairing, he cried out, "*Ribono Shel Olam*, I have no one but You to turn to, no one but You! I beg You, I plead with You, help me, guide me. Tomorrow I will come face to face with the *Satan* again. Only You can help me in my struggle." The tears coursed down his cheeks. He tried once again to focus on the words that swam before him: "The Lord will put to rout before you the enemies who attack you; they will march out against you by a single road, but flee from you by many roads."

His hand trembling, he closed the *Tanach* and pressed it to his lips. "Thank You, *Hashem*, thank You," he whispered before falling into a deep, dreamless sleep.

Wednesday evening, Vlad Stepanovich hitched the horses to his wagon. "We'll be back soon," he assured Katia, and then with a flick of the reins they rattled off.

The priest's lodgings were modest: a two-room house and a small study where Father Peter Fyodorovich Kuskov met them. He invited Vlad Stepanovich to enjoy a glass of tea in the small, adjoining salon, but the peasant stubbornly refused, insisting that he wanted to sit in on the lessons. The priest heaved a sigh of surrender and agreed reluctantly to allow the peasant to remain cloistered with them. Vlad Stepanovich winked at Yankeleh and the boy returned the gesture, and felt heartened.

"Yaakov, would you mind calling me Peter? After all, I am not really all that much older than you are," the priest urged, attempting to put Yankeleh at ease.

"Whatever you prefer," Yankeleh shrugged, trying to ignore the dour gaze of the icon that hung overhead and the stifling aroma of incense that permeated the room.

"Good, very good," the priest grinned warmly. "Now, let's begin with the first Gospel, the Gospel According to Matthew."

Yankeleh's skin prickled and the color drained from his face as he recalled his earlier encounter with that work.

The prelate began reading, his eyes glued to the text. He continued uninterrupted for some twenty minutes, never lifting his eyes from the page. The smooth sound of the priest's voice soon lulled Vlad Stepanovich to sleep. Yankeleh sat listening, rigid and tight-lipped. "Do you have any questions, Yaakov?"

Yankeleh took a deep breath, and shook his head no.

"Every word in this Gospel is clear to you?"

Yankeleh shook his head yes.

"Well, if you understand the meaning of the Gospel, why do you refuse to come into our Church?"

Yankeleh smiled weakly. He preferred to avoid confrontation and did not care to offend the priest, not only out of courtesy for another man's faith, but also for fear of the consequences.

"I understand every word, Peter," he said, using the priest's first name in an effort to disarm him. "But those words are meant for you, for the gentiles. We Jews have a special, unbreakable covenant that the Lord made with us at Sinai, and the Lord our God, King of the universe, does not break His covenant with His people."

Much to Yankeleh's surprise, the priest smiled in reply.

"Well said, Yaakov, well said. You are a very intelligent young man." The priest spread his hands before him. "Next week we will turn to the Gospel According to Mark," he declared without emotion.

Yankeleh shrugged. "Your efforts are wasted on me, Peter. Why bother?" he ventured brazenly.

The priest chuckled. "Well," he said, his palms held upwards, "it is my time to waste, isn't it, Yaakov?"

"That's true."

"Good. Then we shall continue our readings." Rising, he removed a key from his desk and went over to open a closet. Yankeleh sat transfixed. Inside was a full set of the Talmud, just as the priest had promised a week earlier.

"Now that we have finished our lesson, would you care to study a tractate of Talmud with me?"

Yankeleh started. Regaining his composure, he considered the priest's words. Was this a trap? Again he eyed the priest with suspicion. Father Peter Fyodorovich placed a volume on his desk. He motioned for Yankeleh to open it. Overcome with emotion Yankeleh leaned over and kissed the Gemara. With trembling hands, he turned the pages, eager to find the last Gemara he had studied. His eyes glued to the text, he was stirred by a sudden revelation—could it be God's plan for him to teach the priest Talmud in order to soften his heart toward the Jewish people? His pulse quickened. He wondered—is it possible to turn an enemy into a friend? If he could show the priest the beauty of Torah, to make him understand why the Jew is so loyal to his God, why he is ready to face death for *kiddush Hashem,* for the sanctification of His name, maybe he would understand why he should not try to force Jews to leave their faith.

Then, returning to the text, Yankeleh swayed back and forth as he intoned the familiar chant and gazed at the words that he had last seen so long ago. So deeply engrossed was he in study that when the grandfather clock struck ten, he jumped. He rubbed his eyes and glanced at Father Peter Fyodorovich. The priest sat mesmerized, his fingers steepled, his eyes wide.

"I'm sorry," Yankeleh blurted. "I am afraid I was carried away. I had no idea how long I had been studying, nor what time it was," he admitted.

"I understand, Yaakov. But remember, next week we will study together."

Yankeleh nodded uncertainly.

✶   ✶   ✶

The following Wednesday, Vlad Stepanovich once again joined Yankeleh at Father Peter Fyodorovich's home. As before, the peasant refused the priest's hospitality. He remained adamant, insisting that he would not leave the priest's study, and if the priest so wished, he would gladly partake of refreshments, but only within earshot of the lessons. And so, slurping his tea and munching on the cake, he nodded off to sleep, certain that his very presence insured that Yankeleh would not come to harm.

As the weeks went by, the lessons continued. Father Peter Fyodorovich began each week with his readings from the New Testament. He would then close his Bible, replace it on a shelf, remove the Talmud from its padlocked cupboard, and begin learning with Yankeleh. After their first meeting, though, he never again questioned Yankeleh on the portion from the New Testament that he had read, nor did he initiate any discussion on theology. In fact, Yankeleh noticed that the priest seemed almost as eager as he was to get down to the particular Gemara. Although Yankeleh was still young and his formal study had prematurely ended shortly after his thirteenth birthday, he was nonetheless a fine teacher. Soon the two were poring over the text, holding *chavrusah*-style discussions. Some evenings they would empty the samovar before realizing the late hour, the good peasant long since asleep and snoring contentedly.

The months flew by. It was only the onset of winter, and the often steep, impassable snow drifts, that would interfere with their weekly meetings. After so many months of serious study, Yankeleh was convinced of the priest's sincere desire to learn, although there was still the perfunctory reading of a portion of the New Testament. Yankeleh was now certain that the priest meant him no harm, though it took some convincing to satisfy Vlad Stepanovich, who continued to accompany him to the parish. Eventually, the peasant allowed him to saddle up and ride out on his own, but with the proviso that he carry a hunting knife to protect himself against "bandits, and others," as Vlad had put it, his meaning clear. Yankeleh at first resisted carrying the weapon, but Vlad Stepanovich stubbornly insisted.

Though they had spent months studying together, neither Yankeleh nor the priest had opened his heart to the other. But one night, after a particularly difficult Gemara, Peter Fyodorovich leaned back in his threadbare leather chair, sipping a glass of sweet, scalding tea. "You know, Yaakov, all those years at the seminary I was fed incredible fairytales about the Talmud. It was made out to be some kind of Satanic writing spreading poison against Christianity. I have to admit that when I began to study with you, I had no idea what I would discover. Yet, when we began and you were so eager to learn and to teach, I realized that the calumnies I had heard just couldn't be true. After all, if there had been something to hide, you would hardly have agreed to teach me."

Yankeleh shook his head. "Now that I think back, Peter, I shudder when I realize how close I was to adding to those calumnies. You see, I was suspicious of your motives. I thought that maybe you were plotting something devilish against me and my people. And now I realize that had I hesitated to teach you, you would have thought that it was because there was something sinister in the Talmud itself."

The priest poured more tea. "Then tell me, what made you change your mind and agree to teach me?"

Yankeleh rubbed his chin as he considered his answer. "Let's just say that it must have been Divine inspiration."

Peter Fyodorovich grinned broadly and then smacked Yankeleh on the back. "Well said, well said, Yaakov."

"Be careful, Peter. Had Vlad Stepanovich seen you lay a finger on me, he would be at your throat."

The two chuckled.

"You know, Yaakov, I have often wondered why a man like Vlad Stepanovich Ruszky should be so protective of you. It's no secret that he's a drunken brute, and that his poor wife and children suffer from his excessive drinking. So why is he so decent to you?"

Yankeleh sighed and massaged his forehead. "To tell you the truth, he is a very complex man. Who can know what is in the deepest recesses of a man's heart?" he said with eyes lowered, not daring to reveal what Katia Ivanova had confided in him. Even after her revelations there were many questions that remained unanswered. He clasped his hands before him, pursing his lips thoughtfully. "But maybe you know something that could shed some light on the way he acts," Yankeleh probed with tact.

"The truth is that all I know about the Ruszky family comes from local gossip, and as a priest, I don't relish gossip. Still, to be honest, sometimes it is the only way that I learn about the problems facing members of my flock. You see, peasants as a rule are not very open, and unfortunately, they seldom come to me with their problems. So I have learned to listen selectively, and if I feel my help or intervention is needed, I make it my business to visit the family. Of course, I make it appear as if it were just a chance visit." The young priest's brows knitted together.

"Yaakov, how can I describe the pain and misery I encounter on those visits? It's enough to destroy a man's faith. And yet, it is my faith that keeps me from giving up hope for my fellow man. My belief in God gives me the strength to remain here and offer these people some succor. Because, Yaakov, I know in my heart that if they lose their faith, then they have lost everything. And it is because I feel that faith is so important that I worry about Vlad Stepanovich. He seems to have lost his way to God."

Yankeleh sat thoughtfully, and then shook his head no. "I think you're wrong about Vlad Stepanovich. I see in him a spark of humanity, and without faith, I don't believe a man like Vlad could have any humanity left. I see another aspect of the man, an aspect that only those closest to him see. He is a perplexing man: Look at how he treats his children, and yet he is so gentle with his eldest, Marina. In all of the months that I have been with the family, he has never once laid a finger on her. In fact, she seems to bring out the best in him, the best in all of them. He is so very protective of her. Last Christmas he even bought her a pretty comb for her hair. The truth is," he said, shaking his head, perplexed, "that she is very different from everyone in that family. She almost…it's like she doesn't really belong to them."

"It's odd that you should say that, Yaakov. I would not have mentioned this to you if you had not said what you just did. You see, there are stories about Marina."

"What kind of stories?"

"Again, Yaakov, it's just gossip, and one must be wary of gossip."

"Please, Peter, whatever you tell me will go no farther, I promise."

"Very well then. I have heard the villagers say that she is not their natural daughter. It seems that Katia Ivanova was childless for some five years after their marriage. And then one day she appeared in the village with a two-year-old child. When questioned, she said that her cousin had died and she had adopted her child. But some of the villagers seem to doubt her story. And then, miraculously, just a few months after Marina came to live with the family, Katia Ivanova was with child. After the birth of Stashia came the three boys. It seems that Marina brought the family good fortune. That might be the reason for a man like Vlad being so kind to her. He may consider her to be the cause of some kind of Divine protection."

Yankeleh stared ahead, trying to put together a puzzle, but still the pieces would not fit together. "But you don't know for sure whose child she is?"

Peter Fyodorovich shook his head no. "I imagine that the only people who know the truth about Marina are Vlad Stepanovich and his wife, and they may take their secret to the grave with them, I'm afraid."

Yankeleh fell into a thoughtful mood.

"Is something bothering you, Yaakov?"

"I don't know. Your story troubles me, and I just don't know why."

"You could ask them, you know."

Yankeleh considered this for a moment and then shook his head. "I don't think they will tell me the truth. If the truth is to be known, it will have to be found elsewhere," he said sagely.

"Yet," the priest continued, "despite Marina's presence, he still drinks heavily, and he takes out his fury on the rest of his family."

"I think he is bitter over what might have been. He feels helpless, you see. Maybe he would like to be a better provider for his family, and since all he sees is poverty, well, the vodka helps him escape from his despair. You see, Peter, I really think that in his soul he is a God-fearing man, but his faith is not strong enough to help him overcome his disappointment."

Peter Fyodorovich scratched his head, grinning

faintly. "You amaze me, Yaakov. So much wisdom for one so young."

"I may be young in years, Peter, but in one year I have lived many lifetimes."

The priest clasped his hands before him. "Perhaps you wonder why I have never asked you about your experiences as a cantonist, or, as a matter of fact, anything about yourself before you were taken away from your family. It's not that I don't want to know. It's just that in my heart, Yaakov, I admit I am a coward. You see, my young friend, and I think by now I can call you friend, I know that my Church has inflicted so much suffering upon you and upon other innocent Jewish children, and for me to hear it from your lips would cause me too much anguish." He blew his nose noisily with his handkerchief. "I came to my vocation out of love—love of God and love of man. I wanted to be a pastor, to gather together all those lost sheep out there and to give them comfort in this difficult life of ours. I have never lifted my hand against my fellow man, neither physically nor in my heart, Yaakov. Can you believe me?"

Yankeleh nodded. "I do believe you, Peter."

"I learned much in my years at the seminary, not only from the mouths of my teachers, but in the library, where I read and reread history, the Bible, and whatever else I could lay my hands on. Do you know what shocked me more than anything? It was the discovery of my Church's inhumanity to God's own people. When I raised the question in class, the priest shouted out a string of curses about God's pariahs, the rejecters and killers of the savior. But then I would read about Jesus the Jew, born in Bethlehem, raised in Nazareth. And I would return to class, where I was taught to despise his own people. To me, Yaakov, this was blasphemy. But I soon learned to curb my curiosity as well as my tongue, and so I stopped asking and just kept studying on my own."

Yankeleh stared at the man before him, his young brow furrowed. "Then tell me, how can you ask me to join a faith that teaches such hatred against my own people?"

"Have I ever asked you to give up your faith, Yaakov?"

"No, not outright. Yet you read your Bible to me weekly. To what purpose?"

"I don't know," he replied, shaking his head. "I suppose it is to salve my own conscience as a priest. It may be hypocritical, but I, too, am confused. I feel threatened with doubt about who I am and what I stand for, and worse than that, what my own religion stands for." He sighed deeply, and then leaned closer to Yankeleh. "Shall I confess something to you, my young friend?"

Yankeleh sat upright, his eyes open wide.

"When I first met you, that is, after our first meeting here in the parish, I prayed nightly that you would remain steadfast in your faith. Whenever I looked into your troubled eyes, I only saw those terrible welts on your back, and it made me feel rage at my Church. And so I secretly prayed that you would overcome their bestial behavior toward you and that you would not succumb to their beatings and threats." The priest sighed with relief, his burden lightened. "Now that I have admitted this heresy to you, there isn't any need for readings from my Bible. If you like, we can take the time to study the Old Testament together. I always find it comforting to read the Psalms, or any portion that you wish to read."

Yankeleh's face lit up. "Can we begin with *Bereshis*? With Genesis?"

"Whatever you say, Yaakov. But then we have to learn twice a week. One night for Talmud and the other for Bible."

Yankeleh stuck out his hand to his new friend. "Tuesday is the perfect day to learn Bible. Do you know why, Peter?"

The priest combed his fingers through his beard lazily, a glint in his eyes. "Can it be that the third day of the week is twice good?" he smiled, and then before Yankeleh could interject, he continued, "God said: `Let the waters under heaven be gathered into one place, so that dry land may appear'; and so it was. God called the dry land earth, and the gathering of the waters he called seas; and God saw that it was good. Then God said, `Let the earth produce fresh growth, let there be on the earth plants bearing seed, fruit-trees bearing fruit, each with seed according to its kind.' So it was; the earth yielded fresh growth, plants bearing seed according to their kind and trees bearing fruit, each with seed according to its kind; and God saw that it was good. Evening came, and morning came, a third day."

Yankeleh clapped his hands in boyish delight. "You must have been a good student," he beamed.

Peter Fyodorovich smiled broadly in response. "Not too bad, Yaakov, not too bad."

EIGHT

"GET THAT HOG onto the wagon," Vlad Stepanovich shouted as his sons prodded the squealing, ponderous pig with the sharp point of a long stick. They were still unable to convince her to waddle up the ramp.

"Why is that old sow carrying on so?" Yankeleh asked, turning to Vlad as the two loaded the cart with baskets of vegetables and burlap bags of beets and potatoes.

Vlad snorted, "That lazy sow's just too fat to move, that's all. But she's a prize porker, and she'll fetch us a few rubles at the fair." He again turned his attention to the struggling boys. "Come on, use some muscle. Igor, grab her tail. Yuri, you and Volya push. She'll move, you'll see." But the huge pig refused to budge. In desperation, Vlad Stepanovich stomped over, shaking his head. Vlad's quick, sharp whack on her rump sent the hog scurrying up the ramp. He chortled with satisfaction as he rejoined Yankeleh, who was now trying to encourage the squawking, well-fattened geese up onto the cart.

Katia Ivanova and her daughters heaved a huge basket of specially prepared food onto the cart alongside the farm produce. Katia's weeks of sewing, embroidering, and mending now showed: They were all decked out in their holiday best. The boys, as well as Yankeleh and Vlad, wore embroidered, belted shirts, and their pants were tucked into gleaming, well-worn boots. Katia had taken extra care with the brilliantly hued embroidery on the girls' blouses, and now Stashia and Marina giggled with delight as they flounced their petticoated skirts about, their eyes shining with excitement.

Finally, they were ready to go. The sisters clambered up onto the cart, their neatly braided hair framing their fresh faces. Marina sat with her arm about her younger sister, her eyes dancing with anticipation. A gaily patterned kerchief enveloped Katia's head, somehow managing to cheer up her usually somber demeanor. The early morning autumn sun shone with razor sharp clarity, and the air tasted like cognac. Unexpectedly, Vlad Stepanovich's voice rose in song, and soon the whole family joined him in singing beloved folk melodies.

As they took to the main road they were joined by a caravan of other peasants, all decked out in their festive best, singing and joking as they carted off their best crafts, prize animals, and the fruits of their labor to the annual fall fair. With summer at an end and the harvest over, it was time to enjoy a brief respite, to forget daily labors, and to relish a day of infrequent camaraderie. Yankeleh, bronzed, broad-backed and a good head taller than Vlad

Stepanovich insisted on taking over the reins, suggesting that his master lean back and enjoy this fine September day.

By the time they reached the town square of Poshekhonya Volodarsk, which hosted the local spring and autumn fairs, it was already packed with peasants vying for the best spots to exhibit their wares. Here and there arguments broke out into brawls, but by mid-morning order had been restored by the single local police officer. The women began hawking their wares, their raucous voices rising above the clamor. The younger children, eager to spend the few kopeks given to them for sweets, went rushing about, and were soon contentedly munching on buns and sweets. Everything settled into a time-worn pattern. Women and their older daughters proclaimed the virtues of their produce. The older sons extolled the fine qualities of their geese, ducks, chickens, and roosters. The husbands assembled about the pens, where they boasted to one another of the finer points of their respective horses, swine, goats, and cattle.

The barnyard sounds coupled with the shouts of the crowd were exhilarating to fifteen-year-old Yankeleh. He looked more like a man than a boy as he stood with Vlad Stepanovich, encouraging him to hold out for a better price for his prize sow. When Vlad finally sold his hog for what he felt was a fair price, he slapped Yankeleh on the back, and with his arm thrown across Yankeleh's shoulders he strode back to his family. Much to their surprise he generously handed each of his children a few kopeks, encouraging them to go off to enjoy the rest of the day.

Yankeleh had been included in Vlad's largess, and within minutes he had lost himself in the crowd, carried away by the excitement. On one side of the fair, away from the vegetable and livestock vendors and just past the fishmongers, were the artisans: shoemakers, tinkers, weavers, hatters, sack makers, shirt makers, web makers, ironworkers, metalworkers, needleworkers, and every other conceivable craftsman. And there, amongst the craftsmen, were faces from Yankeleh's past, Jewish faces, men in *kapotes*, women with their heads scarved, dark-eyed boys with curled *peyos* and *Yiddishe hittels* running about playing tag, young girls standing at their mothers' sides or engrossed in their own games.

Yankeleh's heart raced. He looked about, glancing at the faces of his people, wanting to approach, to engage someone in conversation, to reveal himself as a fellow Jew. His attempts were met by rebuffs and uneasy glances, however, for his clothing was that of a peasant. He knew they were fearful of his motives, thinking no doubt that this was just another *shaigetz* looking to cause them trouble or to steal their wares. He strolled among the rows of stalls, smiling and nodding, trying to reassure them that he meant no harm. But they were not reassured, and they drew away. There were moments when he was tempted to address them in Yiddish, but something chastened him to hold his tongue.

As he strolled away from the clamor of the crowd he beheld an elderly Jew, almost hidden behind a wagon loaded with bits and pieces of assorted crockery. The man's beard was a fan of white, and his eyes were gentle and mellow. Much to Yankeleh's surprise, instead of drawing away like the others the old Jew smiled at him and beckoned him to come near.

"Come over here, lad. You look like a good boy. So now tell me, young man, what are you looking for? Maybe you want to buy your mother a nice vase for flowers or a teapot?" he suggested, pointing to several ceramic teapots on his stand. "Now, here is something that is sure to please her," he said, holding up a cobalt-blue, glass vase.

Yankeleh smiled faintly. "How much is the teapot?" he asked timidly.

The old man returned his smile. "Ah, you see, I am a good judge of character. You are a good lad; I could see it in your eyes. Now let's see, for mothers we have special prices. This pot is usually ten kopeks, but for your mother, eight kopeks."

Yankeleh looked down at the coins Vlad had given him. He shook his head, showing the old Jew the five kopeks he held in the palm of his hand.

"Ach, well, you must have a very good mother for her to be blessed with such a fine son. I will let you have the teapot at a loss. Five kopeks it is," he said, handing the teapot to Yankeleh.

Yankeleh handed the old man the coins. He stood there for a moment, hesitating, and then, taking a deep breath, addressed the man in Yiddish. "*Ich bin a Yid*, I am a Jew."

The old man stared, too shocked to speak.

"I am a cantonist," Yankeleh continued, his voice a breathless whisper. "I was kidnapped two years ago. I work on a nearby farm…" His voice caught, he found it difficult to continue.

The old man pressed his hands to his mouth and stared into Yankeleh's face. "*Guttenyu*," he exclaimed, "you look like a *shaigetz*, a *muzhik*. I never would have guessed. Yet I saw something in your eyes that made me call you over. And even as I called to you, I wondered what made me do such a foolish thing, since most of the *shkutzim* come here looking for sport. I swear to you, it is the first time I have ever done such a thing. Yet something in my heart…," he said, shaking his head, still unbelieving. "But who are you? Where are you from?"

"My name is Yaakov Yitzchak Halevi from Kronitz Podolsk."

Before Yankeleh could utter another word, the man grabbed him. He looked stricken. "You…you are the Kronitzer Rebbe's son? *Gut in himmel*! I cannot believe my eyes." And then, in an agonized whisper, he asked, "Are you still a Jew? There were rumors that you had become a *goy*, that you were baptized."

"God forbid!" Yankeleh cried out. "I am a Jew, and I will go to my grave a Jew," he exclaimed, his face reddening with anger. "They have spread this rumor to entrap Jewish children in their net, to dishearten them and to weaken their resistance."

The old Jew smiled, relieved, his face suddenly radiant. Extending his hand, the man blurted, "*Sholom aleichem*. I am Lazar Farbstein from Volodya, a poor man as you see, but rich in joy that I've lived to see you this day."

Yankeleh grasped the man's gnarled hand. And then he frowned, shaking his head in distress. "Reb Farbstein, I fear that this calumny against me may have reached my father's ears. I beg you, is it possible for me to find someone to write to my father, to reassure him of my loyalty to my people, and to tell him where I am and that I am well? Maybe the rabbi of your town? Perhaps he could contact my parents—and give me the strength, the *chizuk* that I so long for?" The boy's voice broke. "I have been alone…so alone."

"The rabbi?" he said, nodding his head in thought. "Yes, I see that you must meet with him. But it is dangerous. You must promise me to be very cautious. The Czar is a demon and his men are always on the lookout for boys trying to escape. They come to the *kahals* sometimes searching for some poor lad who managed to run away. Very few escape. Most are found and…" he covered his eyes with his hands as if to blot out this terrible vision. "But the rabbi cannot come to you, and how will you ever get to Volodya?"

"My master permits me to use his horse, and I have Sunday afternoons to myself."

"*Baruch Hashem*! But you will still have to be careful, not only for yourself, but for the Jews in the town. This is a dangerous business," he said, shaking his head. He then scratched his ear as he considered the consequences. "Look, my boy, are you certain that you can get away next Sunday and come to the synagogue in Volodya?"

"I will be there," Yankeleh reassured him.

"Good. Then just remember that the synagogue

is two blocks west of the town square. Our rabbi, Rav Duvid Malinsky, is a great scholar and a *tzaddik*. He will be waiting for you there. Yes, yes," he muttered, his eyes gleaming, "you must see him. All I ask of you is that you use great caution. Do not reveal yourself to anyone, not even to the *shammas* or the *gabbai*. And remember, no matter who speaks to you, you are to reply only in Russian. You will pretend that you understand no other language. Do I make myself clear, Yaakov Yitzchak? If anyone asks what you want, say that you have been given a personal message for the rabbi. Perhaps dressed as you are no one will suspect." He placed his hand on Yankeleh's arm. "But listen carefully. It is fortunate that you have come to speak to me. There are always informers about who can do you harm. I beg you, I know it will be difficult, but do not speak to anyone else here today. The fewer people who know about you, the safer it will be for you," he warned, his eyes mirroring his fear.

"But…I don't understand. You mean there are Jews here who would harm another Jew?" he muttered.

"Are there *khappers* who kidnap Jewish children, Yaakov Yitzchak? You should know," he answered with a deep sigh.

Yankeleh shivered, gripped by the terrible memory and a sudden sadness.

"Now tell me, my dear child, are you all right? Are you treated well?"

"Thank God, I am quite well now. The peasant I live with is a decent man, and I have no complaints. He even gave me a few kopeks to spend—this teapot is for his wife, a good woman who has been very kind to me. And for all of this I am grateful to the Almighty. What the future holds for me, I cannot know, but this I do know, and this I vow: whether I serve in the Czar's army one day or twenty-five years, I will remain a Jew and I will return to my village."

Reb Lazar Farbstein wiped his eyes and then blew his nose noisily with a huge, red handkerchief. Glancing about to ascertain that no one was watching, he placed both his hands on Yankeleh's head. "May the Lord bless you and keep you, Yaakov Yitzchak," he said gruffly, his eyes brimming with tears. And then, with a hint of a smile, he handed Yankeleh back his five kopeks. "Go, have a fine time," he said warmly, patting Yankeleh's shoulder.

Yankeleh thanked Reb Lazar Farbstein and bid him farewell. Though the fair was still animated with people, and flags still fluttered in the breeze, everything suddenly seemed subdued to Yankeleh. Nostalgia overcame him, and he longed with growing fervor for home and for his parents. He made his way through the crowd, no longer admiring the wares or looking into the smiling faces of the milling men, women, and children.

A scream ended his reverie. Yankeleh stopped in his tracks. Quaking, he recoiled as he heard the sound of a cracking whip followed by screams and moans. He forced his way through the knot of people huddled in curiosity about a whip-wielding peasant who stood, legs apart, over a cowering boy. Yankeleh stared in horror. His stomach knotted, bile rose to his mouth. He couldn't breathe as he looked into the tortured eyes of his friend Srulik. The peasant continued beating Srulik mercilessly until he fell to the ground, curled into a shuddering human ball. And then, as if for good measure, the peasant spat and kicked Srulik in the ribs. "I warned you, yid, to guard the pigs. Now don't move from here again," he growled, stalking off.

Yankeleh stared at his friend in growing horror. He wanted to rush over, to comfort him. Trembling he stared at Srulik, a mass of bruises and welts, his face twisted in pain. Yankeleh remained rooted in his place, too overcome to move. He had to think, to regain his composure. He glanced about, and only when the peasant was well out of sight and the crowd had moved on to other amusements did Yankeleh find the courage to approach his old friend.

"Srulik!" he cried, as the boy slowly stumbled to his feet.

Srulik stiffened. He pulled away from Yankeleh, his eyes wide with terror. And then he gasped and threw his arms about Yankeleh's neck, weeping unashamedly.

"Srulik, Srulik, my friend," Yankeleh said, over and over again.

"Yankeleh," he whimpered, trying to stem the tide of tears. "Forgive me, I…I almost didn't recognize you." Yankeleh pulled back to stare at his friend. The boy's face was haggard, with one eye partially closed and swollen. His Russian peasant's clothing hung on a lanky frame. But worst of all was the bleak look of despair in his eyes.

"What have they done to you? Are they trying to kill you?" he blurted out.

Srulik bit his lip. "You don't know the half of it. They

are beasts, him and his sons, beasts. They have made my life one long hell. They starve me, they beat me. All I pray for is death. It is my only hope of escape," he said forlornly. "You don't know what it's like living with such animals. It makes even Kirov seem like heaven," he said with bitter irony.

Yankeleh drew his friend into the shadows. "Listen to me. You have to try to get away."

"Oh, Yankeleh, that's all I dream of, but death will be my only escape. I wish they'd finish me off and be done with it," he moaned. "That's all I think about and pray for, day and night—escape, escape from this horrible life."

Yankeleh turned his head away to hide his emotions. There had to be a way out. If Srulik were to remain, his end would be death; that much was clear. "Srulik, you have to get away from there."

"There is no way out. Believe me, I know," he groaned. "I have heard enough stories about boys like me who tried to escape. They set the dogs upon them."

"No, no, there has to be a way out for you," Yankeleh said, rubbing his forehead. He turned and looked into his friend's eyes. "Srulik," he murmured, "I know it's a gamble, but we have no choice. Just listen carefully," he said, lowering his voice to a whisper. "Next Tuesday, sometime after midnight, I'm coming for you."

"You're insane. They have the barn padlocked. I can't get out."

"Srulik, there has to be a way out of the barn. Every barn has an opening in the hayloft. After midnight, climb up to the loft and watch out for me. When you see me, jump. Don't wait for any signal, just get out. You'll ride back with me. I'll try to work out some kind of a plan by next week, and, as God is my witness, with the help of God I'll get you out of this hell."

"No, Yankeleh, I can't let you do this. It's too dangerous. You'll get caught, and then what will you have accomplished? No one can get close to the farm without waking the dogs, and they make enough noise to wake the dead," he lamented.

"Leave the dogs to me. I know how to deal with them. A few scraps of meat will keep them quiet."

A trembling Srulik shook his head. "I don't know. It's no good. It'll never work. They'll come hunting for us and then we'll both be doomed. It's too dangerous, Yankeleh. I can't let you do it."

"Srulik, just trust me. All I know is that you have to get away before they kill you. I'll work something out. Just be ready next Tuesday." He embraced Srulik and rushed away, his face knotted with anguish.

He quickly headed back to the Ruszkys' stall. He greeted Katia with a heavy heart.

"Is something wrong, Yaakov?" she asked.

"No, nothing," he replied, forcing a smile as he handed the teapot to her.

She gasped. "Yaakov, you shouldn't have spent your few kopeks on me," she said, her voice warm with pleasure.

"You have been so good to me, Katia Ivanova, it's just a small way of my saying thank you," he said with a sincerity he felt deeply.

He insisted on joining her in outshouting the other vendors, all the while formulating ways of escape for his friend Srulik. But first he would speak to the rabbi in Volodya. Perhaps the solution would be found with him.

✴   ✴   ✴

With the excuse that his back pained him, Yankeleh asked Vlad if he could leave early Sunday morning to visit the doctor in Volodya. Certain that Yankeleh's back pain was the result of the beatings he had received, he readily agreed. Yankeleh saddled up at the break of dawn, eager to arrive in Volodya before sunset.

It was a long journey. When an exhausted Yankeleh finally entered the town of Volodya, he was rejuvenated by what was, to him, a wondrous place. He gaped at the stately, solid brick homes on tree-lined, cobblestoned streets. Those who passed him winked at one another and laughed at the young, callow peasant awed by their modest town.

Fortunately, Lazar Farbstein's directions enabled him to find the synagogue with ease. He dismounted in front of the impressive stone building. A large menorah was beautifully engraved over the entrance. It was the most magnificent synagogue Yankeleh had ever seen. He led his mount to a nearby trough and tied him securely to a post before heading to the synagogue. Though it was still too early for evening prayers, Yankeleh nonetheless hoped that a few worshipers would be about. With trembling hands he opened the heavy, wooden door and went in. Peering into the semi-darkness, he saw a figure silhouetted against the gloom. The man turned and then rose slowly. As his eyes grew accustomed to the dim light, he knew without doubt that the distinguished looking man approaching him was Rabbi Duvid Malinsky.

No words were exchanged. Rabbi Malinsky drew Yankeleh toward him in a heartfelt embrace. Then, taking him by the hand, he led him to a far corner of the large room. The rabbi was a slight man, just past his middle years, and even in the lightless room Yankeleh could see wisdom reflected in his eyes.

Rabbi Malinsky indicated for Yankeleh to be seated on one of the benches. He gazed at Yankeleh for a long time. When at last he spoke, his voice was strangled with emotion. "When Lazar Farbstein told me of his meeting with you, and when he repeated the words you uttered to him, I..." he cleared his throat, "it was a moment I shall never forget. For days I have prayed fervently that nothing would keep you from coming here today, and now I am grateful to the Almighty that He has answered my prayers and that Yaakov Yitzchak Halevi is actually seated here before me." He stroked his full, black beard, streaked with silver, with long delicate fingers. "In my mind I have written and rewritten a letter to your father, waiting only to see you before setting down my thoughts in writing. We must thank God that you are one of the few who fell in with decent people."

Yankeleh nodded his head and licked his dry lips. He was almost too overwhelmed to speak. "Rabbi," he finally said, "my parents—I must write to them." Now the words came out in a rush. "And if I can get a pair of *tefillin,* and a *siddur,* and..."

Rabbi Malinsky laid a comforting hand on the boy's shoulder. "All in good time, my son," he said softly. He glanced out the small window at the gathering darkness. "It is too late to put on *tefillin* now. My rebbetzin awaits you with a fine Jewish meal. Then we will have plenty of time to take care of everything."

The rabbi took Yankeleh by the hand and led him to his modest though pleasant home.

The rebbetzin beamed with joy at the sight of him, and within minutes a memorable feast was set before Yankeleh, a meal that had been for Yankeleh a distant dream, a memory of a childhood lost. After washing and reciting the *HaMotzie*, and enjoying the warmth of freshly baked bread, Yankeleh stared in disbelief at the platter of gefilte fish set before him. Surely this huge serving of fish was not meant only for him! But the look on the rebbetzin's face made it clear to Yankeleh that he was their only guest. The fish was followed by a huge helping of Shabbos cholent that had been set aside for him. He sighed with pleasure as he sank his fork into the fat chunks of flanken, the rich, brown potatoes and beans, and the peppery kugel. He insisted that he could not eat another bite, when a portion of roast goose was set before him. Somehow he managed to devour that, too. After savoring every forkful he sank back in satiated exhaustion, too stuffed to partake of the generous slices of sponge and honey cake the rebbetzin now insisted he must at least taste.

The conversation during dinner was limited to exclamations of delight at the rebbetzin's culinary skill. After dinner Yankeleh followed the rabbi into his study.

Rabbi Malinsky sat down at his desk and wrote words of explanation to the Kronitzer Rebbe, and then Yankeleh lovingly added his own message, expressing his love for his parents and his devotion to Torah.

The letter sealed, the rabbi gently urged Yankeleh to talk about his life as a cantonist. As the story unfolded, the rabbi sat immobile, his eyes clouded with pain and, at times, filled with horror. Only when Yankeleh eased out of the past and into the present did both manage an occasional smile. Finally having told someone about his experiences a huge weight was lifted from Yankeleh's shoulders, and he breathed a sigh of relief.

The rabbi and Yankeleh stopped to sip tea and nibble some of the rebbetzin's pastries. Yankeleh then repeated his earlier request for a pair of *tefillin*. The rabbi immediately walked over to his cupboard and took out his second pair of *tefillin*, handing them to the startled boy. His hand trembled as he held the precious objects.

"Are these your *tefillin*, Rabbi?"

The rabbi smiled warmly. "They were here waiting for you, my child."

The hour was growing late, and there were still pieces of a puzzle that Yankeleh wanted to set into place. Holding the *tefillin* tightly, he edged closer to the rabbi.

"Rabbi Malinsky, may I ask you a question?"

The rabbi smiled warmly and spread his hands in submission.

"I hope you won't think my question strange. You see, since I have been living with the Ruszky family, something has been troubling me. I was hoping that you might shed some light on the family. That is, I would like to know if you know something about their daughter Marina," he probed.

The rabbi seemed perplexed and somewhat disturbed. "Tell me, Yankeleh, why are you interested in learning about their daughter?"

Yankeleh spoke slowly, trying to piece together his thoughts and feelings. He began by describing how very different she seemed to be from the rest of her family, not only in appearance, but in her behavior. He also confided the story of her adoption as told to him by the priest, Father Peter Kuskov.

"You know, Yankeleh, there are so many peasant families in this region, and we Jews have very little to do with them," he said, gazing into Yankeleh's eyes. "But I will admit that I have heard of the Ruszky family."

Yankeleh's brow knitted as he leaned forward.

"It is a very long story," the rabbi began. "In fact, it started about the time you were born, in a village not too far from where the Ruszkys now farm. There were about fifty Jewish families living there—good people." He paused thoughtfully, then continued. "The *goyim* in the village lived in peace with the Jews, until one day, it was before their Easter holiday, a pack of bandits from another town rampaged through the village. There was a terrible pogrom. Everyone...every Jew was killed, men, women, and children," he said, his voice quivering. "A year later, the doctor from Volodya was summoned to the Ruszky farm. It seemed that the wife was having a difficult labor and the old midwife had sent the husband here for him. Fortunately for all, a healthy baby girl was born, and the wife, despite the difficult delivery, was also fine. When the doctor returned he came to me with a bizarre story. He told me that the Ruszkys had a three-year-old daughter, a cousin's child whom they claimed to have adopted. But for some reason, the doctor didn't believe their story. His doubts led him to call on the village priest, a Father Yusup, whom he treated from time to time. It was from Father Yusup that he ferreted out what we now know about the child. After much prodding, and I imagine a bribe, the priest confessed to the doctor that Marina was, in fact, Miriam, the daughter of the village *melamed.*"

Yankeleh's jaw dropped and the blood drained from his face.

The rabbi continued, "It seems that Katia Ivanova and her husband worked for several Jewish families in that village. They were known to be an honest, hard working couple. According to Father Yusup, they had rushed to the home of the *melamed* to help him, only to find that they were too late. We can assume that the child's parents had hidden their daughter, and that the Ruszkys found her. The couple had been married some five years and were still childless, so they decided to take the child and bring her up as their own. To protect themselves and the child, they invented the story of a deceased cousin. But Father Yusup admitted that he, too, doubted their tale and had gone so far as to check up on the extended family. He discovered that no such cousin existed. He then told the doctor that he had confronted the couple and revealed to them that he knew who the child's true parents were, suggesting to them that the child be baptized. But he said they stubbornly stuck by their story and insisted that the child had already been baptized by her parents."

Yankeleh sat rigid, listening in stunned silence.

The rabbi continued, his face drawn. "The moment I heard the doctor's story, I rushed to see the Ruszky family. I pleaded with them to return the child to her people now that they had a daughter of their own. I even offered a substantial sum of money in the hope of convincing them to give up the girl. But nothing helped; my pleas were fruitless. They insisted that their adopted daughter had brought them good fortune, and nothing I could say or do would convince them to give her up. They even threatened me with bodily harm—and worse, they threatened to stir up the *goyim* against the Jews of Volodya if I persisted in my efforts to take the child from them. So you see, my son, there was little that we could do without endangering our community. It was a difficult decision, but after a long discussion, the *kahal* decided not to press the issue."

The rabbi leaned back and studied Yankeleh for a long moment. His brow knitted, he bent closer to Yankeleh. "What I have to say now I know will be difficult for you to understand, but I must ask you not to utter a word about this to anyone. This secret must be locked away in your heart for the sake of all of the Jews here."

"Marina knows nothing about this?"

The rabbi shook his head sadly. "She knows nothing."

Yankeleh leaped to his feet. "But then I must tell her. She must know."

The rabbi indicated for him to be seated. "Yankeleh, listen carefully. You must do nothing to endanger yourself or the Jews here. Keep in mind that there is an entire Jewish community to think of. And as much as we all want Marina to return to our people, you have to consider the consequences of your actions."

Yankeleh sank back into his seat, desolate.

"Believe me, my son," the rabbi said, placing his hand on Yankeleh's arm, "we have considered every alternative. Maybe one day…" he sighed deeply, "maybe one day there will be a way. But now promise me that you will not betray my trust."

Yankeleh reluctantly gave his promise. He then drew himself upright. Though the story of Marina had come as a shock, he had another mission to carry out. He now edged his chair closer to the rabbi and poured out the story of his friend Srulik. Finally, he described his plan to help his friend escape.

Rabbi Malinsky grew agitated. He held up his hand in a warning gesture. "What you plan to do is careless— worse than careless, it is dangerous for everyone concerned. You must realize that the very first place the authorities will search is the Ruszky farm. They know full well that you two had been friends. Do you take them for fools?"

Yankeleh bit his lip. "Then maybe I can bring him here?" he proclaimed, his eyes brimming with hope.

"*Chas v' chalilah,*" the rabbi gasped, horrified. "Hear me out, my son. Please do not think me hard-hearted. But you must understand these are very difficult times for us," he said, shaking his head. "The slightest incident can cause disaster for all of us. We must be extremely cautious. Your friend's lot is a bitter one, true, but he has endured much, and with God's help he will survive this test, too. You saw him when he was beaten and miserable, but no doubt there are better times, too. I know you want to save your friend, but once again I must remind you to consider the consequences of your actions. There is nothing I can do, nothing that anyone here dares to do. You must forget your plan. It is far too dangerous," he pleaded.

Yankeleh rose shakily. Pointing an accusing finger at the rabbi, he blurted, "First it is Marina, and then it's my friend Srulik. How can you live with your conscience?" he sobbed.

"Yankeleh, I beg you, calm yourself," the rabbi pleaded. "My son, I know you are a compassionate young man, and that is how you should be. But one day, when God wills it, you will step into your father's shoes, and only then, Yankeleh, will you understand my pain. Do you think I have no heart, no compassion? Do you think I do not bleed for every Jewish soul? But I have to think of the thousands of Jews who are entrusted to my care. One wrong word, one wrong step, and their lives are forfeited. That is the reality of life under Czar Nicholas. And so I have to make these decisions, these terrible choices. I pray that you never will be placed in such a position. But you must try to understand."

It was a confused and troubled Yankeleh who embraced the rabbi and took a tearful leave.

During his long journey home, he weighed the rabbi's words, considering his warning. By the time he wearily arrived home, a golden ribbon of light stretched across the horizon. He heaved a deep sigh as he dismounted, his decision now made.

NINE

THE PALE SUN filtered through a white winter sky and a cold wind lifted dead leaves as Yankeleh attempted to concentrate on mending a fence. Though Igor worked at his side, there was meager conversation between them; both seemed absorbed in their own worlds. Yankeleh glanced up at the sky and shuddered. Winter was fast approaching and the taste of snow was already in the air.

He waited eagerly for the pale rays of the late autumn sun to sink into the horizon. As the stars emerged diamond bright, Yankeleh raced back to wash, daven, and wolf down his supper before dashing off for Tuesday evening study with Father Peter Fyodorovich Kuskov. Once again he reviewed his plan. At an early point in the evening he would pretend to feel ill, in the hope that he could abruptly end their usual leisurely hours of uninterrupted learning. It was vital that he begin his journey to Ivan Alexeivich's farm at about 10:00 p.m. According to the strategy he had mapped out he would arrive at the farm somewhat before 1:00 a.m., giving him ample time to return home well before sunrise.

As Yankeleh galloped toward the church, he had to admit that the priest had made these past few months the happiest he had known in a long time. Father Peter had given him the opportunity to learn again, and oddly enough, he found learning with Peter to be exciting. The young priest had a sharp and probing mind, and in response to his hunger for knowledge, they had covered much ground in the Talmud, a good part of it new to Yankeleh. At the priest's urging, they had also expanded their learning to include Chumash and *Nach*. Had it not been for Peter's clerical robes, Yankeleh could easily have forgotten that he was in fact a priest of the Holy Russian Orthodox Church. They now studied together in *chavrusah* fashion, with the priest imitating Yankeleh's sing-song intonation, swaying along with him as they reviewed a gemara. With a sigh, Yankeleh wondered where this would all lead. But that answer would come much later. For the present, Yankeleh had other concerns.

Father Peter drummed his fingers impatiently, eager to begin their study session. When Yankeleh entered, Peter wasted no time in amenities—the Bible was already on his desk, opened to the chapter they were to study that evening. Yankeleh cleared his throat as he bent over the text and pursed his lips, ready to read and to explicate. But as the words leaped out at him, his voice caught. He shivered. It was as if the Hand of Providence were pointing the way: "David got up from behind the mound and bowed humbly three times. Then they kissed one another and shed tears together, until David's grief was even greater than Yonason's. Yonason said to David: `Go in safety; we have pledged each other in the name of the Lord, Who is witness forever between you and me and between your descendants and mine.' "

Yankeleh read the words slowly, quietly, half to himself. And then, lost in a world of his own, he sat silent, almost oblivious to the priest's presence. Finally Peter spoke. "Is something troubling you, Yaakov?"

Yankeleh bit his lip, wanting more than anything to unburden himself. Instead, he shook his head no. He rose hastily, his knees shaking, his face flushed. "Forgive me, Peter, I guess I was just overcome by the thought of such a deep friendship," he said, trying to control his trembling. "Besides, I'm just not feeling well tonight. If you don't mind, I'd like to head back home."

"If you'll give me a minute, I'll go and change and take you back, Yaakov. You don't look up to riding alone," Peter declared, rising from his seat hastily.

The color drained from Yankeleh's face. He tried to avoid Peter's piercing gaze. "No, no, I'll manage fine. Besides, the gallop home in the cold air will clear my head," he said with a reassuring smile. "In fact, I'm feeling better already." He pulled on his coat and wrapped the woolen scarf about his neck. "I'll see you tomorrow," he assured him, with forced cheer, as he dashed from the study.

Father Peter sank into his chair, his brow creased

with worry. He considered whether to ignore Yankeleh's protests and follow him. Reflecting briefly on Yankeleh's odd behavior, he shook his head and grinned slightly. "Adolescent sickness," he muttered to himself as he returned to the text.

Over the past week, Yankeleh had traced and retraced the route to Ivan Alexeivich's farm in his mind. He had made subtle inquiries from Vlad about the man and his family. From afar he had observed the spread of the farm, the barn, and the variety and number of livestock, taking every aspect of the countryside and lay of the land into account as he worked out his plan of rescue. Now as he urged his horse on, Yankeleh, for the hundredth time, reviewed his plan. Despite the rabbi's pleas and warnings, Yankeleh knew he could not rest until Srulik was safely out of the grasp of the beast Ivan Alexeivich.

He had begun hatching his plan on the very night of his return from Volodya. At first he thought he would reveal his plan to Vlad and ask him for help. He knew Vlad pretty well by now, and he trusted him, yet he realized that he would be compromising this simple man and would be placing him and his family in grave danger. He then wondered whether he should confide in Peter. This, too, he rejected. Although he had grown to like Peter as a friend, still he could not forget that Peter Fyodorovich Kuskov was, after all, a priest, and he could not be certain of his intentions. He had to find another way.

On his return from Volodya, physically and emotionally drained from the trip and the encounter with the rabbi, Yankeleh explained to a concerned Vlad that the doctor had insisted that he must return for a second visit. "The doctor says he has to make up some kind of an herbal remedy," Yankeleh said with a frown, shaking his head solemnly. "I told the man that I couldn't possibly return, since it would mean leaving my master early on Sunday again, and I had my duties to attend to."

"What do you mean not return?" Vlad growled. "You go next Sunday, and that's an order from your master," he bellowed.

Yankeleh could not conceal his joy, and he impulsively threw his arms around Vlad, "Thank you, Vlad," he said sincerely.

A startled and embarrassed Vlad Stepanovich tramped off, shaking his head and muttering.

The following Sunday Yankeleh awakened before dawn and raced to Volodya in search of Lazar Farbstein, the kindly old Jew he had met at the fair. It wasn't too difficult to find his housewares shop in the Jewish section of Volodya. The tiny shop peered out from a shadowy corner of the dirt-paved street, showing a ramshackle face to the world. Yankeleh pushed open the creaky door, peering into the musty shop filled with a jumble of crockery. Lazar Farbstein was alone, a *sefer* in hand, his eyes closed in prayer. The old man had not looked up as he entered. Yankeleh waited with growing impatience for Lazar Farbstein to turn his attention to his potential customer. At the sight of Yankeleh, Lazar Farbstein jumped to his feet, his jaw dropping in amazement.

"Yaakov Yitzchak ben Moshe Halevi?"

Yankeleh smiled at the old man's full pronouncement of his name.

"What...what are you doing here?" Lazar Farbstein stuttered.

"Can we talk privately?" he inquired.

"Privately?" Farbstein chuckled. "You cannot get more private than in this shop. But look at you, you must be exhausted from your journey. Come along. I will close the store for a while. We will go home. I am a childless widower, and so we will be very much alone, I am afraid."

Lazar Farbstein's home was, in fact, a shabby, sparsely furnished shed attached to his shop. After washing, the two shared a modest meal of black bread, cheese, and tea. Only then did Yankeleh discuss his plan with Lazar Farbstein. Reb Lazar stared at him in shocked silence for several long minutes. Finally he spoke.

"Yaakov Yitzchak, what you propose is sheer insanity. Do you realize how dangerous such a mission can be? Now tell me the truth, has the rabbi sanctioned such a course of action?"

Yankeleh had no need to reply. His eyes spoke for him.

"The rabbi has shared his wisdom with me, and I know it is wrong to disobey. And yet, I believe that if the rabbi were to understand the true gravity of my friend's situation, he might reconsider. But I just can't stand by and watch my friend being slowly torn to shreds by beasts," he exclaimed tearfully. "Reb Lazar, I ask you, could you abandon your friend to certain death if there were even a thread of a chance to save him?"

The old man rubbed his chin in thought. "To be honest with you, maybe I would have the courage to risk my life, but the lives of others…" he said, shaking his head, "I don't know. I really don't know."

"You don't know only because you are not faced with this problem. I am sure that you would move heaven and earth to save your friend, as I am willing to do now. But I admit I cannot do it without help, and I need your help now."

"What do you wish of me? What can I do?" he asked.

"I need a safe place to hide my friend, at least for a while, until I can think of a plan to get him out of Russia."

Lazar Farbstein gestured at Yankeleh with his bony hand. "How long do you think one can hide someone in these times without being discovered, my boy? People have tongues—anything unusual, even the purchase of more food than usual, can cause gossip. And then what? How long will your friend be safe with me?"

"I beg you, help me, help save a Jewish child, Reb Lazar," Yankeleh cried. "Reb Lazar, you know it is written that we don't have the right to sit back and wait for the *Ribono Shel Olam* to make things happen for us. If we begin, then God will help us." His voice grew forlorn. "Is there no Jew left who will help the cantonists?"

Lazar Farbstein wiped his damp eyes with a huge handkerchief. Slowly he murmured, "Perhaps there is a way."

Yankeleh clenched his fists tightly and held his breath as he waited for Farbstein to speak.

"But it all depends on another man, a good friend of mine. I will ride out tomorrow to see him, and I'll come to your farm with my answer."

"What is the plan?" Yankeleh asked eagerly.

Lazar Farbstein replied in a low voice. "I have a friend, an itinerant peddler. He lives about twenty-five miles from the farm of Ivan Alexeivich, in a *shtetl* with a few dozen Jewish families. He himself has four children, and one more mouth to feed would not be obvious to outsiders. He is a good, honest, and decent man. Comes spring and Gershom Lader is off on his travels, which take him to St. Petersburg and sometimes even farther, all the way to Lithuania. He sells cloth, pots and pans, dishes, little trinkets for the children, and all kinds of tools and farm equipment. From him I buy housewares for my shop, and over the years we've become good friends. But good friend or not, the question is whether he would be willing to risk his life to hide your friend until spring. By spring the authorities will have ended their search. And then, if all has gone well, he would have to take your friend along with him, keeping him hidden until well out of this district, you understand. From St. Petersburg, there is always a chance that he, or perhaps someone he trusts, would take the lad on to Lithuania, where he would have to be smuggled across the border. It's very complicated and risky, Yankeleh. But the way I see it, it's your friend's only hope."

Yankeleh leaned forward, his eyes bright with expectation. "That sounds like a wonderful plan."

Lazar Farbstein licked his lips nervously. "Yankeleh, a plan is only a plan if all the parties agree to it. I cannot speak for Gershom, but I do promise to go out to see him. You will have my answer tomorrow evening."

✶   ✶   ✶

The night was black, the moon and stars veiled by clouds. Yankeleh could depend only on his sense of direction and his instinct to guide him to his destination. With his knife as his only protection, Yankeleh drove his horse with reckless abandon, his heart racing. The howling of jackals and wolves roaming the forest in search of prey filled the air, seeming to encircle him. The low branches whipped his face and body, making the way painful and at times treacherous. His panting, sweating horse slowed to a canter and then to a wary lope as they approached the farm. With the scraps of meat that he had scavenged in hand, Yankeleh guided the steed toward the barn, flinging the stuff in all directions to keep the roaming hounds at bay and quiet. His luck held—they greedily devoured the spoils, their voices never raised to announce the intruder.

As he slowly approached the barn, Yankeleh heard a muffled sound as something dropped to the floor. His eyes, now adjusted to the pitch darkness, made out a skeletal specter covered in rags. Yankeleh leaned down and pulled the form onto the horse, and with the thin arms about his waist, raced back toward the forest.

They had galloped for several miles before Yankeleh pulled the horse to a halt. He had to speak to Srulik, to explain the plan. His pulse racing and his mouth dry, he managed with difficulty to speak to his friend.

"Srulik, are you all right?"

"A little nervous, but otherwise fine," his friend replied, with a trace of his old jauntiness. "The truth is,

Yankeleh, I never thought you'd do it. You know this is *meshugga*. We'll never get away."

"Listen to me. We don't have the luxury to discuss the merits of this adventure," Yankeleh said, affecting an equally carefree tone. "Just be quiet and listen to the plan," he instructed.

When he had finished, Srulik let out a deep gasp.

"How'd you ever manage anything like that?"

"One day," Yankeleh murmured, managing a low chuckle, "when we have lots of time, I'll share the details. Now we have to be on our way."

"One moment," Srulik said insistently. "Why me? This is your chance to escape, Yankeleh."

Yankeleh paused. The thought had passed through his mind, oh how many times. "My friend," he whispered, "for two of us to escape would only compound the danger to us, to our accomplices, and to the Jewish community here. Now, it is you who are in mortal danger if you remain; I, on the other hand, can survive as a Jew. No, this is your chance; someday, mine will come." Grimly, he spurred his horse and off they sped.

The village was silent, though an occasional howling dog served to quicken Yankeleh's pulse. Meticulously instructed, Yankeleh found Gershom Lader's dwelling without difficulty. Yankeleh had no need to dismount. A tall, muscular man awaited them, and before Yankeleh could steady his horse, the man lifted the frail Srulik and carried him off into the darkness of the small cottage. There was no word of parting, just a touch of their fingertips. Yankeleh whispered a prayer of thanks as he spurred his horse homeward, arriving as the cock announced the coming of dawn. He walked the snorting, sweating horse to his stall. After grooming the animal he huddled under the covers, unable to stem his sudden uncontrollable shivering. Yankeleh fell into a deep, fitful sleep, only to be shaken awake by Vlad, who stood over him, his eyes wide with worry.

TEN

SRULIK'S VERTEBRAE STABBED Gershom ben Naphtali Lader's arm as he cradled the frail boy. He gazed down at him, a deep, painful sigh escaping. Stealthily, he carried Srulik down into a musty cellar, feeling his way in the pitch darkness with practiced sureness.

Srulik clung to this stranger who seemed to have emerged from nowhere to offer him refuge. He peered into the velvet darkness, making out silhouettes of boxes and barrels. It struck Srulik that they were heading toward a brick wall. He blinked several times—were his eyes deceiving him? The tall, powerfully built man rubbed a niche in the wall. What had looked like a solid wall creaked open. Srulik fought back a cry. Gershom stepped beyond the wall and motioned for Srulik to follow. He then bent over and lit a kerosene lamp. In the warm glow of light, Srulik saw what appeared to be a storeroom piled high with farm equipment, wooden casks, barrels, and stacks of wooden cases.

Gershom stared at Srulik and then muttered, "This will be our little secret, yes? You see, it's how I protect my family and my merchandise during a pogrom." He hesitated, and then clearing his throat, he added, "And also how I protect my special guests."

Srulik drew in a deep breath and then followed him into the shadows. Hidden behind the piles of farm equipment was still another room. The rugged-faced man removed a key from a hidden recess in the wall and opened the rusty padlock. He then lit the lantern in the room, and Srulik released a loud gasp. The room was small and windowless, though Srulik could feel a flow of fresh air coming from an unseen vent. Cramped into its space was a bed, an upholstered chair, and, to Srulik's astonishment, a shelf with *seforim*. He swept his gaze around the small room—his eyes fell on a pair of *tefillin,* writing paper, a pen, and an inkstand resting on a table near the shelves. A screen concealed a tub and wash basin. It seemed to Srulik that the room contained everything one might need for an extended stay. Though the room was meticulously clean, Srulik knew that he was not the first to be afforded its protection.

In his excitement, he at first had not noticed a covered platter on the table, but the tantalizing aroma soon engaged his senses. Srulik licked his lips in anticipation, staring eagerly at the man at his side. A smile surfaced as Gershom Lader extended his hand and introduced himself formally. "I'm afraid, Yisroel, that this will have to do for the present," he said sympathetically. Then the smile broadened. Pointing to the covered platter, he added, "My wife, Itkeh, thought you just might be hungry after your long midnight ride."

Though bewildered, Srulik returned the smile. For the first time in a very long while, he felt the tension ease from his body. There was something about Gershom Lader's manner that was reassuring.

"One thing I can assure you, you won't go hungry here," Gershom declared. "I suggest that after you've eaten, you get a good night's rest. My Itkeh will be down in the morning with breakfast, and I will try to come by later in the day," he said kindly. "I am afraid your questions will have to wait until then, Yisroel. For the present you are safe here. But you must remember, if you hear any sound, you are to remain absolutely silent. No moving about, no eating or drinking…and almost no breathing. Do you understand?"

Srulik nodded his comprehension.

Gershom Lader's wife, Itkeh, rose long before the rest of her household. There was always too much to be done and too little time to do it, she would complain. She began her morning chores, placing loaves of dough into the oven, preparing feed for the chickens, and washing the milking buckets for her seven-year-old Avigail, who was already a good milker. Then she prepared her family's morning meal.

On this day especially she dare not tarry. It was imperative that her hidden guest be fed before the rest of the family rose. It had been agreed between Gershom and herself that, out of consideration for their safety, the children never discover the cellar sanctuary. She moved with great haste. Only after she checked that the children were still fast asleep did she venture into the cellar with the platter of eggs, white cheese, jam, freshly baked bread, and an urn of steaming tea. She tapped on the door and called out his name. Srulik sat bolt upright, confused. Where was he? And then, with a deep sigh of relief, he fell back onto the pillow. He rubbed the sleep from his eyes and then rose to open the door a crack.

"I am Reb Gershom's wife. No need to worry," she assured him in a whisper, her smile encouraging. She set the platter down and cleared the table of the leftovers from the night before. She then gazed at the undernourished, grime-covered boy, a pained expression on her face. She nodded toward the screen.

"Reb Gershom will be down shortly to fill the tub with hot water and bring some clean clothing." A deep sigh of sympathy escaped her lips. "Now don't you worry. You will see, in a short time we will put some flesh on your bones."

"I…I just don't know how to thank you and your husband," Srulik muttered, longing to find the words to express his gratitude.

"Shh, no need for that," she said, placing her finger to her lips. "You are a *Yiddishe neshamah*, and we are only doing what must be done. Reb Gershom will explain the situation to you. For the present, rest, and when you regain your strength, you can read and study. It will help pass the time, and it is good for the soul," she declared, pointing to the *seforim* on the shelf.

The aroma of freshly baked bread floated through the pleasant cottage as Reb Gershom and the children, their morning prayers completed, sat down to relish the first meal of the day. Pinchas, the eldest, sat next to his father. He was just sixteen, and though well-built, he was short and stocky, unlike his father, with a prominent nose and bright, dark brown eyes. Binyamin, an energetic and wiry fourteen-year-old, sat alongside. The eleven-year-old, still pudgy Feivel, and a freckle-faced and pigtailed seven-year-old daughter, Avigail, both sat opposite. Gershom leaned back and embraced his beautiful children with his gaze. In the six months of the year that he spent with them—those precious six months—he did his utmost to make up for the time they were fatherless.

It pained him that his dear Itkeh had to carry so heavy a burden of responsibility, rearing the children alone for half the year. As the years passed, he remembered his parents with gratitude for having the wisdom to find him so wonderful a wife, a wife who had stood by him during all of these trial-filled years. Itkeh, the daughter of Daniel and Basha Leiteizen, was a woman of strong character who administered her household with a firm and judicious hand. She even managed to organize his less than orderly business records, while keeping a keen eye on his accounts. He thanked God daily for his good fortune, while accepting God's will in all things, even those that caused pain. For no matter how many years had passed, the terrible agony of having lost his firstborn son, his beautiful Yosef, brought tears to his eyes. "My first born, my *b'chor*," he thought, "taken in the bloom of childhood." He swallowed a sigh, his eyes fixed upon the platter of fresh eggs before him. Still, there were many blessings for which to be grateful. He had four beautiful children, and in the spring, his eldest son would be joining him in his travels, along with another, he remembered with apprehension.

Where had the years gone? he mused. It seemed that only yesterday he had been drawn into his strange occupation. He had learned from his father, an itinerant peddler, how to respond to the challenges of the road: to defend himself from the anti-Semites ready to attack and cut his throat for sport, to be on guard for the highwaymen on the prowl for illegal gain. His father had been a good teacher and had taught Gershom the tactics of survival. He reminded himself that, despite the many dangers of his profession, his father, thank God, had died safely in his own bed at the ripe age of eighty-three. Gershom's father had imparted to him the rules of survival in business as well. "Be honest, my son," his father had cautioned. "Your good name is worth more than money. Give value, be ethical, and you will garner profit for yourself and for your people." In fact, it was his father's reputation for ethical business dealings and honesty that had served Gershom well in those early years.

The young and energetic Gershom soon expanded his father's route, which had originated from their home in Martynovich. Slowly he headed northeastward, and after his marriage, he managed to obtain permission to settle in a *shtetl* not many miles from Kirov. This new location enabled him to venture farther north to Finland

and west to Lithuania. He also expanded his father's inventory, which had mostly included housewares, cutlery, textiles and notions, and had added tools and farm equipment.

But the real metamorphosis came about much later and almost by accident. He numbered among his customers peasants, artisans, merchants, and several heads of the local *kahals,* among them Reb Shlomo Alter ben Aryeh, a man of considerable wealth and prominence. Gershom knew that Reb Shlomo Alter did business with him more out of friendship than out of need. It was over a steaming glass of tea one late spring afternoon that Reb Shlomo Alter casually asked Gershom if he would be willing to perform a mitzvah. He then confided that he needed a large sum of money to be delivered to Rav Avraham Moshe ben Shlomo, a *rosh yeshiva* in Vilna. Rav Avraham Moshe, he went on to say, was a leading Lithuanian Torah light, and the money would be used to support and enlarge his yeshiva and to provide much needed help for destitute students. Gershom agreed. In truth he felt honored that Reb Shlomo Alter would entrust him with such a mission, although he knew full well the danger of travelling with large sums of money. Still, he had long admired Reb Shlomo Alter as a charitable man who devoted his life to the good of the Jewish community, and for so important a person to place his faith and trust in him was a singular honor.

When Gershom arrived in Vilna and handed the money over to Rav Avraham Moshe, he recalled how the rabbi had dabbed the tears from his eyes and had blessed him. Rav Avraham Moshe then asked Gershom if he would be willing to undertake another difficult task. The rabbi stressed that this particular mission was of great importance, and he could only commend such important documents to someone he believed to be absolutely trustworthy. When Gershom agreed, the rabbi handed him a packet of papers containing, as he found out only later, evidence that would exonerate a prominent rabbi of charges that certain anti-Semites had made before the authorities.

Some time later, Reb Shlomo Alter suggested to Gershom that, in addition to serving as courier, he could perform a great service to the far-flung Jewish communities by bringing them information that might prove useful to them. In those early years, Gershom saw nothing unique in his role as messenger for the *kahals* and rabbinic authorities. Only much later did his role expand from simple messenger and bearer of minor tidbits of gossip to somthing far more important. His friendship with members of the police, which he had nurtured over the years, bore fruit and enabled him to provide significant information to the *kahals*. In time, his contacts expanded to include leading Torah authorities throughout Russia and Lithuania.

It was during this period of transformation to courier-agent under the guise of peddler that he was asked if his home could be used as a safe haven for the occasional runaway conscript or deserting Jewish soldier. He consented with the proviso that his wife agree. It was understood that his home would be used only in the most urgent situations, so as not to endanger his family or compromise his role on behalf of the Jewish community at large. Itkeh assented, despite the danger. "There is nothing more important than saving a Jewish life," she had declared with the courage of a virtuous woman.

With Yisroel now tucked safely away in the cellar, Reb Gershom girded himself against the onslaught that he knew was about to come. Ivan Alexeivich's farm was too close to their *shtetl* for comfort, and it was inevitable that the police would soon be pounding at his door in search of the runaway. This was not the first time, and though Gershom was adept at handling the police and the army, there was always an element of the unexpected, and therefore an element of danger.

It was as he anticipated. The boys left for study, and Itkeh and Avigail went to the market, leaving Gershom alone in the quiet house. With a grim smile he soon heard the persistent pounding on the door announcing unwelcome guests.

Gershom forced a smile as he opened the door, ready to bid the officer in charge welcome. He tried to hide his dismay as he stared into the face of a new man. It was not the easygoing Vanya Ilyavich who faced him, but a red-faced, sneering sergeant.

"We're looking for a runaway cantonist," the police officer growled.

"Oh, I see," Gershom replied, his hand on his cheek in feigned commiseration. "Well, what can I do for you, Sergeant?"

"Out of my way, Jew," he spat out.

Gershom nodded. "Of course. You are welcome to come in," he replied with exaggerated courtesy.

A bottle of vodka had been strategically placed on the table, and, as the men roamed through the cottage, Gershom offered Sergeant Yuri Vasilovich Vasig a drink, which was readily accepted.

"Nothing here," a private muttered.

"Look in the cellar, you clods!" the sergeant barked.

"You are a clever fellow, Sergeant," Gershom responded with tight control.

Gershom lit a kerosene lamp and opened the trap door. Several men descended into the murky darkness, their eyes hungrily scanning the stock. Gershom picked up several trinkets along the way, along with a bolt of cotton cloth.

As they exited, he handed each of the men a trinket, exclaiming with a wink that he knew they would want something for their wives or girlfriends. The bolt of cotton cloth he handed to the sergeant, who was smiling broadly.

"Sorry to have bothered you," the sergeant called out, tipping his hat as they made their way out.

Gershom sank into his chair, mopping the perspiration rolling down his face and neck. He was grateful that Itkeh was out doing her morning marketing. He hated to subject his wife and family to such ordeals. Now he hoped they would leave him in peace.

When Itkeh returned, she gazed about the room and then at her husband. "They were here?"

"How can you tell?"

She threw her hands in the air. "I can smell them,"

she said mockingly. "So?"

"The sergeant with them was a new man. I never saw him before," he said, shaking his head. "But I took care of them—a few trinkets, a bolt of cloth, nothing too much. Just enough to keep them happy and away."

Itkeh sighed deeply. "When will this all end?"

"God only knows, my dear wife. But in the meantime, we do what we must do."

"Have you been down to see the boy?"

"No, not yet. It is a very difficult situation, Itkeh. The boy has to stay put for at least seven months. Seven months in a cellar," he shuddered, rolling his eyes skyward. "Such a punishment on the poor child."

"Do you have a choice? It is better here than by that *bulvan* Ivan Alexeivich. I couldn't believe my eyes. Have you seen that child? A bag of bones."

Gershom sat with his hand on his forehead. "But how will the boy manage in such a prison for so many months?" he muttered almost to himself. "Still, maybe we could let him out in the middle of the night for a breath of air and some exercise."

"Later, Gershom," Itkeh shook her head, her expression wary. "It would be far too dangerous now. You never know who is watching. One of the *goyim* might be on the lookout. Who knows?"

"You are right. But it will be hard on the lad, very hard."

Before the children returned that evening. Gershom

descended into the cellar to visit Srulik. He helped the boy scrub away the accumulated grime, refilling the tub several times.

"So now we see a face," Gershom chuckled as Srulik donned fresh, clean clothing.

"You and your good wife have been so kind to me," Srulik said eventually. "How can I ever thank you enough?"

Gershom released a long sigh. "Look here, my boy, the ordeal for you is only beginning. You know the police are combing the district. They have already visited me, and I have a feeling they will return. It is a ticklish business, you see. They won't rest until they find a runaway cantonist, for fear that a successful escape will encourage others. But I assure you that others have escaped—not many, but there have been some lucky few. The path is difficult. One must be very careful, very circumspect," he warned. "Yisroel, you seem to be an intelligent lad. Do you understand what I am trying to say to you?"

Srulik stared at the man seated opposite him, not quite comprehending. He shook his head. "Yes and no," he admitted.

Gershom pulled at his beard nervously. He did not want to upset the lad. Still, he had to be forthright. "You see, Yisroel, I am a peddler by profession, and the only way we can get you away safely is to have you join me when I begin my travels," he began. "I leave here in the spring, right after Pesach." He then looked searchingly into Srulik's eyes. "You do know what time of the year this is, Yisroel?"

Srulik nodded. "Just past the *Yomim Noraim*."

"That's right. Now do you understand what I mean?"

Srulik nodded weakly. "I will have to stay here, here in the cellar, until spring," he said, his eyes filming over.

"Yes, Yisroel. I am afraid so."

Srulik grinned faintly, and then shrugged philosophically.

"Anything is better than spending one day with Ivan Alexeivich."

Gershom chuckled, placing his hand encouragingly on Srulik's arm. "That's a sensible lad. You'll see, it won't be all that bad. There is plenty to read and study here. It will give you time to rest, to regain your strength and put some flesh on those bones. You will need stamina for the journey ahead. And when things quiet down, maybe we will get you out for a breath of fresh air and even some exercise, all right?"

Srulik nodded, his eyes bright with gratitude.

It was before midnight when hammering on the door and shouts drove Gershom and Itkeh from bed. They glanced at one another, unable to hide their alarm. Putting on his robe, Gershom rushed bleary-eyed into the kitchen. He unlatched the door and found himself staring into the leathery face of a seasoned army sergeant.

"Where's the boy?" he barked menacingly.

"What boy?"

"The runaway cantonist, yid," he shouted, the veins in his neck pulsating.

"Ah, that boy," Gershom replied remotely. "The police were here yesterday. I take it they haven't found him as yet," he shrugged.

"Don't play the fool with me."

Gershom tried to hide the contempt he felt. "I am sorry, sir, but you woke us from sleep, and I know nothing about this boy. It is easy enough to check. You are free to come in and look around. I have nothing whatever to hide, I assure you," he said in a placating tone. "You can ask anyone around here. I am a law-abiding man."

"Then keep the law in mind, Jew. If you hear of anyone sheltering the runaway, you report it immediately," he said, stabbing his finger into Gershom's chest. "And besides, yid, there's reward money out. That should ease your guilty conscience," he hissed.

It was with difficulty that Gershom concealed his fury.

A glass of steaming tea and some mandelbroit were already on the table before Gershom shut the door. He sat down in silence, his heart thundering. He tried to sip the tea to ease the tightness in his throat.

"It will be all right, Gershom," his wife comforted him. "But we must be on our guard. Maybe they suspect something. Who can know?"

Gershom threw his hands up in derision. "They know nothing. They are just trying to frighten us. Ach, it's a game, Itkeh. They really think they're so clever."

"But how can you be so sure?" she pressed.

"My dear wife, believe me when I tell you that I

have had enough experience with those people to know how they think and how their minds work. It's a piece of theater, and that is all. Now you must promise me never to react to their threats. You must remain calm at all times."

"I don't know. He seemed so sure of himself."

"Itkeh, listen to me. Use your *sechel*. If he had suspected anything, do you know what he would have done? He would have ordered his men to tear this house apart. You think these are fine people? I assure you, they know nothing, nothing at all."

She shook her head, her expression thoughtful. "I suppose you are right, I suppose you are right," she repeated to reassure herself.

The police and army visits continued for over a month. Only then did the matter appear to be put to rest, although Gershom and Itkeh remained on guard, and Srulik was kept secluded within the confines of his room. "I don't trust them," Gershom declared. "I still think they have their eye on this village. They are just waiting for a chance to pounce."

It was particularly difficult for Itkeh. She had to manage her household as if all were normal, all the while knowing that hidden in the bowels of her home was a runaway cantonist, wanted by what appeared to be all of the Czar's minions. Though the tiny hidden room had before been occupied by fugitives, they had never attempted to hold someone for more than a few days. And now, they had to conceal the boy for over half a year!

Out of consideration for the safety of their children,

Gershom could spend little time with Srulik. During the first difficult weeks Srulik paced the length and breadth of the small room, lonely and apprehensive. One day, though, his glance listlessly fell on the bookshelf. He remembered the days when he and Yankeleh would learn together and find comfort; he remembered his own stated desire to go to school. He picked up a *sefer*—and the room was no longer a prison to him.

On one particularly bitter February night, in the pitch darkness of the waning moon, Gershom motioned for Srulik to follow him upstairs. For the first time in four months, Srulik was outdoors. He stepped out into the cold and took a deep breath of the bracing night air. Gershom encouraged him to stomp about, and he dug his boots into the crunching snow.

"I feel like an old man," Srulik whispered, complaining that every part of his body creaked and groaned.

During the next two months they repeated these outings from time to time. But Gershom remained on guard, and so they ventured out only on the murkiest and most uninviting nights.

One night, Srulik reluctantly returned to his room after his precious midnight outing. He removed his coat and gloves, pounded his hands and stamped his feet to remove the last sting of frost. How he relished these nights, despite the biting, icy blasts. Just to smell the fresh, cold air, to look up at the bright, shimmering stars, revitalized his spirits. A glass of steaming tea awaited him, and he smiled at Gershom's thoughtfulness. He drank slowly, savoring its warmth through the sweetness of a cube of sugar held between his teeth, contemplating his good fortune.

Warmed by the tea, he lay down on his cot and closed his eyes, hoping that sleep would overtake him. His thoughts turned again to Yankeleh, and his heart filled with love for the friend who had risked his life to save him from death. He longed to see him, to look into his face and thank him for his devotion and loyal friendship. But Gershom had explained that in order to protect everyone involved in this rescue, no such meeting was possible.

"Believe me, Srulik, your friend knows how you feel. Words between good friends aren't always needed for understanding," he assured him. And yet, Srulik wanted to see his friend, to thank him, to say what was in his heart. He sighed as he remembered how their friendship began. Now, staring into the darkness, he repeated the vow he had made on the very first day he found himself in the safety of Gershom and Itkeh Lader's home. "*Ribono Shel Olam*," he murmured softly, his voice trembling, "if it is Your will that I continue in life, I vow that I shall devote my life to Your laws and Your people. I will study, I will learn, and then I will travel far and wide and spread Your Torah, even to the four corners of the world." And having repeated this vow, Srulik fell into a deep, untroubled sleep.

Itkeh watched the snow melt into the ground as winter's white cloak slowly disappeared. The meandering stream near their home now thundered and roared, and the nearby lake overflowed its shores. She delighted in the warming sun, which would soon bring new life from the earth. She contemplated the change of seasons with mixed emotions, however, for with spring came the agony of separation from her beloved husband. She had long resigned herself to this reality, knowing full well that there was little choice. It was their *parnasah*, she mused. Though the years should have inured her to the months of loneliness, in truth, she still suffered them with anguish.

Now she was grateful that Pesach was approaching and, for the moment at least, she could immerse herself in scrubbing her home. Later, she would be busy preparing her often praised Pesach specialties. Her furious industriousness served to conceal the longing that already wedged itself into her heart. The children giggled as she shouted at them to bring more boiling water and soap, knowing full well that she was not truly angry with them. When very young, they understood that her annual burst of energy was connected to the holiday. As they grew older, they sensed that it was their father's imminenet departure that caused it. They, too, missed their father, and they easily empathized with their mother's melancholy.

Itkeh rushed about checking how thoroughly Avigail and Feivel were cleaning the bedrooms and looking in on Binyamin in the barn. No one in her household was exempt from the chore of removing every vestige of *chametz* from their cottage and its environs. She supervised every step, and now, rubbing her hands dry, she walked into the sitting room to see whether Pinchas was being meticulous in cleaning the *sfarim*, her hands on her hips in feigned disapproval. Pinchas eyed her as he opened each book, shaking it with care and then wiping the covers clean. Only when satisfied that he was, indeed, being properly attentive to his task did she return to the kitchen to continue with her own work. Despite her scolding, the house was a cheerful place, and Itkeh could not help but sigh with contentment.

While she worked, she thought again of Srulik. Though hidden from view, he was never forgotten by Itkeh. Whenever she thought of him behind those four walls, unable to participate in their *simchos*, tears came to her eyes. She was determined to do whatever she could, however, to enable that poor boy to share the joy of Pesach with them. She would prepare a *seder* plate for him, and at least, she mused, he would be able to conduct his own *sedorim* and enjoy the savory feast she was planning. This thought offered Itkeh a small measure of comfort.

The six harnessed steeds pawed the ground, snorting nervously, eager to be on their way. Gershom bid a tearful farewell to his children and his wife. Pinchas, accompanying his father for the first time, was already perched high on the bulging wagon, waiting impatiently to wave goodbye to his family.

Gershom had come for Srulik before dawn, long before the rest of the family had awakened. "This is the most difficult and dangerous time for all of us, Yisroel," he confided. "We will have to be very careful."

"Does your son Pinchas know about me?"

"For the moment he knows nothing," he confessed. "I will only tell him about you and the hiding place when we are well out of the district of Kirov. Then you will be able to join us. Just remember, if anyone asks, you are my nephew Motel ben Shaike Gutman from Martynovich."

Srulik lay silent beneath layers of tarpaulin, girding himself for the second stage of his struggle for survival. He muttered a prayer for everyone's safety and tried to stop the chattering of his teeth on this warm, clear spring day.

ELEVEN

GERSHOM HELD THE reins lightly, glancing sideways at his son from time to time. Pinchas, he mused, reminded him so much of himself at the same age. The young man was seated upright, his eyes wide with wonder and alert with anticipation. Despite the danger, Gershom always found the open road exhilarating, and after all of these years, he still relished the excitement of his work. Now at last he would share part of the adventure with his son. Not that it didn't pain him to leave his wife and children. He missed them terribly already. How he would laugh when Itkeh chided him about his gypsy spirit! Yet he had to admit that it was good to be back on the open road.

He thought of Srulik and shook his head sadly, hoping that the boy wasn't too uncomfortable. He had weighed the options and had decided that Srulik would have to remain hidden for a few days. Instinct told him that it was too dangerous to reveal Srulik's presence even to Pinchas. He had no doubt that the police and army were still looking for the boy.

The slant of the sun's rays reminded Gershom that it was time for prayer. He pulled the wagon over to a rushing brook and fed and watered the horses. They davened Mincha and then sat down under a broad-branched sycamore to enjoy their afternoon meal. Gershom reflected with a flicker of a smile that his wife's provisions could sustain an army. Itkeh had stored an ample supply of food in the wagon for Srulik as well. Gershom glanced at the wagon, hoping that Srulik remembered his admonition to eat only when they were on the road. The wagon's movement and noise, he had explained, would prevent detection. He had also warned Srulik that he could only leave the wagon when Pinchas was asleep. It was still another prison for the lad, Gershom brooded. He mopped his brow, though the air was still brisk. Gershom knew that the danger had not passed. He could not relax until they were well away from the district.

For the present he would concentrate on teaching Pinchas the first lesson of survival in a hostile world, as his father had taught him. Returning to the wagon, he turned to Pinchas, a creased brow forming a frown. "Tell me, my son, how do you feel now that we are together on the road?"

Pinchas leaned forward and gazed at his father. "I feel good. That is, I feel proud to be with you. It's as if I have left childhood behind and I am now an adult," he said. "I feel that you must trust me to take me along with you."

Gershom nodded, and then patted his son's shoulder. "Yes, Pinchas, I do trust you. And that trust will shortly be tested, but for the moment I want to know whether you have ever wondered how your Poppa manages to survive in this business. You must realize by now that there is always danger lurking on the open road."

Pinchas smiled. "I'm no fool, Poppa," he replied, his eyes taking in the full measure of his father. "You are big and strong. I guess the bandits are just afraid to bother you."

Gershom chuckled. "I wish it were so simple, Pinchas. Muscles won't protect a man against knives and revolvers, I'm afraid."

Gershom's words struck a note of fear in Pinchas, and he winced, the color draining from his face.

"Survival, my son, in this perilous world that we live in is solely in God's hands. But He wishes us to do our part, to do our best, and that takes a combination of intelligence, alertness, and, unfortunately, the need to protect oneself with other means."

Pinchas's expression mirrored his curiosity. "What do you mean by other means?"

"I will show you, Pinchas." Gershom leaned over and pressed the rise of their seat. A panel opened, and he drew out a revolver and a long-bladed knife.

Pinchas gasped. "B…but Poppa, it's against the law to carry a weapon."

"My son, the first thing a man must learn is that outlaws are just that: they do not keep the law. And for an honest man to survive in such a jungle, he must be able to face the opponent on equal footing," he explained patiently. "When the enemy feels matched or bettered, he often will back away."

He handed the long-barreled revolver to his son. The boy's hand trembled, almost dropping the weapon.

"Pinchas, you said that I took you with me because I could trust you, because you had crossed the threshold from childhood into manhood. Isn't that what you just said?"

Pinchas cleared his throat and nodded shamefacedly.

"Good. Do you still feel you want to continue this journey? If not, it is not too late to turn back. I will not force you to do anything that you do not wish to do."

After a moment's reflection he nodded. "I am a man, Poppa. And I am ready to learn," he said, his jaw jutting out with determination.

"Are you certain?"

"Yes, I am," he replied with assurance.

"Poppa, have you ever killed a man?" Pinchas asked, handing the gun back to his father.

Gershom flicked the reins, staring ahead. "There were times in my travels when I was forced to pull the trigger in self-defense," he murmured, drawing in a deep breath. "And I did not wait around long enough to find out whether my aim was accurate or not." He considered his next words for a moment. "But Pinchas, remember, too, that survival is not merely a matter of might. It takes far more than a revolver and a knife to assure survival."

Pinchas hunched closer. "How else then, Poppa?"

"Ah, you want to learn everything on the first day on the road? Be patient, and be observant, and you will soon see that there are times when using one's head can be as effective, and certainly much safer, than using a weapon," he said sagely.

Pinchas considered his father's words. He clasped his hands behind his neck, leaning back and closing his eyes. "Poppa, thank you for taking me with you."

Gershom threw his arm around Pinchas's shoulders and pulled him toward him, kissing his brow. "We'll be a good team, Pinchas. But remember, we have a long and hard journey ahead."

Pinchas nodded, his eyes shining.

The route they followed had been well marked by Gershom as the safest possible one. Over the years, Gershom had studied the terrain with care and had developed a sort of sixth sense; he had discovered many alternate routes and used them when he sensed danger. Whenever possible, he spent the night with Jewish families, padlocking the wagon in their barns or stables. Only when such accommodation was not possible would he spend the night in the open, or at an inn, after bribing the innkeeper handsomely to protect his merchandise.

After three days on the road, the time had come for revelation. As they rode through Vytegra, Gershom pulled on his gloves and karakul hat. He steered the wagon into a densely wooded area, and they were soon hidden by the wild, thick foliage. He jumped from the wagon and told Pinchas they were making camp out of doors that night.

"But Poppa, it's too cold," Pinchas whined between chattering teeth.

Gershom laughed. "Fresh air will do you good, Pinchas. Remember, inns are not always available to a traveler. One has to find safe alternatives for the night. I know that this forest frightens away the faint-hearted, so it's a good place for us."

Pinchas watched wide-eyed as his father pitched a tent-like structure. He placed a tarpaulin on the damp, mossy ground, and over that he piled three down-filled quilts sewn up into bags. "Momma's idea," Gershom exclaimed, pointing to the sleeping bags with pride. "It keeps the cold out, believe me." Pinchas stamped his feet and pounded his hands together as he watched his father prepare the camp for the night. Before the last vestige of light had disappeared, Gershom piled branches one upon the other and with patience he encouraged a flame, which soon turned into a warming fire. Gershom stoked and fanned the flames until satisfied. He then pyramided stones and mud into a makeshift oven. Pinchas stared open-mouthed in wonder at his father's skills. A nearby brook provided them with water for drinking, washing and cooking.

"Before we daven Maariv, Pinchas, come, sit down here next to me. I want to share something with you."

Pinchas hunched down next to his father, holding his hands over the fire.

"In a few minutes I will introduce you to a very brave young man."

Pinchas looked at his father, incredulous.

Gershom unfolded the story of Srulik's rescue, describing the hiding place in the cellar of their home. Pinchas listened in stunned silence.

"Motel," he called out, using Srulik's new name, the one he would use until he was safely out of Russia.

A well bundled Srulik scrambled from the wagon. He stretched his arms and stamped his feet to rid himself of the stiffness of hours of minimal movement.

"Motel, my boy, I want you to meet my son Pinchas."

Pinchas stared in mute astonishment at Srulik.

Gershom smiled broadly at both of them. "For the sake of safety, Pinchas, our young friend here will be known to you and to everyone else as my nephew Motel, the son of my sister Rivkeh and her husband, Shaike Gutman from Martynovich. Come now, Pinchas, shake hands with your cousin," he laughed.

The boys shook hands perfunctorily, shy smiles surfacing.

"All right, now let's wash and daven," he declared, clapping Srulik on the back. "And then the two of you will learn how to prepare a meal in an outdoor oven," he winked, stomping off toward the brook.

At the first light of dawn the boys were awakened.

"We have to use the time we have wisely," he exclaimed to the bleary-eyed boys. "There are lessons to be learned today, and we have no time to waste."

After praying and eating a quick meal, Gershom removed the revolver from its hiding place. The first lesson began.

Using whatever target the forest provided, Gershom taught Pinchas to aim accurately. Pinchas's hand trembled as he held the revolver. He had not anticipated resistance from the trigger and the revolver jerked from his hand after his first shot. But with practice, he gained a measure of control over the weapon, and on occasion even managed to hit the target.

Dawn had turned into morning, and it was time to move on. For the rest of the way the boys chatted amiably, getting to know one another. Srulik described his life as a cantonist to a shocked Pinchas, although he avoided describing some of the more brutal aspects of his years as a conscript. By evening, the boys had become fast friends.

Over the next few weeks, Pinchas managed to learn some of the elements of good salesmanship.

"You see, Pinchas, it's not enough to open up the wagon and produce merchandise. A good peddler becomes a confidant of his customer. He shares a funny story, or tales of the outside world. In other words, a good peddler is a traveling newspaper. Of course, the object is always to make a sale. But to the customer, that sale is often of secondary importance."

Pinchas and Srulik laughed.

"I know, it looks easy. But salesmanship is an art, a profession like any other. There are skills even in selling a bolt of cloth or a pot," he said with a broad grin. "Remember our visit to Pavel Vasilovich, when he insisted that he had a good spade and he didn't need another. What did I do?"

Pinchas shrugged.

"Ah, then you weren't watching or listening. The first thing I did was to examine his old spade. The bottom was rusted, and so I scraped away some of the rust. The steel was thinning, with a bit more effort there would have been a hole. Now, to have made a hole would be damaging someone else's property," he said with a frown. "But one needn't go so far. Just the hint that within days the spade would be worthless was enough to convince Pavel Vasilovich that it was time to buy a new one."

The boys grinned, their eyes bright with admiration.

The next few months passed quickly, and as spring relaxed its cool grasp and summer's sultry weather wrapped them in its warmth, the three eased into the unique, binding camaraderie of the road. Not once, however, throughout their long travels did Pinchas realize that his father was anything more than a peddler, though Gershom had deftly managed to garner information from his regular sources and report what was pertinent to his contacts with the skill that came from years of experience. They were drawing near the border of Lithuania, and Gershom felt that it was time to reveal to Srulik the next stage of his plan. With Pinchas asleep in the back of the wagon, the two had the infrequent opportunity to be alone.

"When we get to the border you and Pinchas will be introduced to the guards," Gershom explained. "Since I am known to them, there should be no problem. They are well taken care of, you can be sure. Once we are in Lithuania you will stay with old friends of mine, Misha and Fanya

Erlichman. They live about forty miles from Vilna and they are prepared to let you stay with them for as long as necessary. They are good people. And since their children are now all married they are delighted to have a fine young man with them to fill the emptiness of their home."

Srulik's eyes were lidded in thought. He turned to Gershom. "I want to confide something in you, Reb Gershom," he muttered.

Gershom put his finger to his lips, which were creased into a frown. "Remember, I am Uncle Gershom now," he chided.

Srulik nodded. "Uncle Gershom, I am not much with words, but I just want to tell you how much I appreciate what you and your wife have done for me," he said hoarsely, covering his face with both hands.

"Come, my boy," Gershom muttered, placing his arm across Srulik's shoulder. "No need for that. Itkeh and I know how you feel."

Srulik wiped the tears from his face with the back of his hand, pulled out a handkerchief and wiped his brow. In a few moments he regained his composure. "You will thank your wife for me?" he continued, his voice still hoarse.

"Of course, of course, my boy."

He then leaned over, chin on fist. "And there is another thing, Uncle Gershom."

Gershom edged closer.

"All those months that I was hidden in your home, it gave me time to think and to study. And I made a vow."

"A vow?"

"I vowed that if I survived this ordeal I would go to a yeshiva and study," he reddened, turning his gaze away, "and then if God wills it, I would travel the world over to teach my fellow Jews."

Gershom stared at the boy next to him, his eyes misty. He cleared his throat and spoke.

"I will discuss this with the Erlichmans, Srulik. I know that their eldest son, Menasheh, is a *rosh yeshiva*, and perhaps he can find a place for you."

Srulik stammered a heartfelt thank you.

They were just miles from the border when night forced them into the nearest inn.

"Not my favorite place," Gershom admitted somewhat uneasily. "The innkeeper is a surly sort. Oh, he knows me, and he takes my money nicely. But there is something about him that makes me uncomfortable. Ach, well, let's not tarry. Tomorrow is a big day," he said with a broad smile.

Much to the boys' surprise, the innkeeper, Ivan Feodorvich, greeted Gershom as an old friend, his smile leeringly friendly.

"Ale all around?" he urged.

Gershom nodded.

"I'll have my son take care of the horses and wagons. No need to worry, my good friend," he smirked, rubbing his hands together.

"Just remember, Ivan Feodorvich, lock the stall!"

"Ach, come now, Gershom, you know me. Nothing

to worry about," he assured, pounding Gershom on the back. "So these are your sons?"

"My son Pinchas, and my nephew Motel," Gershom muttered indifferently.

"You can be proud of your father, Pinchas. He's a good man, a real good man," the innkeeper fawned, smacking his lips.

"I don't like him," Pinchas whispered when he had tramped off.

"You're right, he's a sly fellow, that one."

The inn was noisy and heavy with the smell of unwashed humanity. Pinchas and Srulik were uncomfortable in the alien atmosphere. They quaffed the ale quickly and headed for the stairs.

Once inside the room Gershom quietly told the boys to remain dressed. He took the bedding and arranged it to look as if they were asleep. He put his finger to his lips and drew them back into the shadows behind the door.

"Pinchas, did you see something unusual downstairs?"

Pinchas shook his head no.

"Always keep your eyes open, Pinchas. Take nothing for granted," he instructed. "When Ivan Feodorvich left us he headed for the back of the room. He was in deep conversation with four men, and he glanced our way once or twice. I know those four well. They are known as highwaymen. He peered out the window. "Come over here, Pinchas. What do you see?"

"The stalls aren't locked."

"Correct. Those men plan to rob us, and our horses are still in harness. Now listen to me," he said, pulling out his revolver and knife. "Tonight you will have your first real lesson in survival," he said. "Pinchas, you hold the knife."

Pinchas shuddered. "What do I do?"

"You'll know when the time comes. Meanwhile just be quiet and watch me carefully."

He turned to Srulik. "You just stay put in that corner."

"But why can't I help?"

"Just do as I say," he instructed.

Srulik licked his dry lips, trying not to shiver.

In a matter of hours the raucous shouts and drunken laughter faded. The three stood silent and alert in the darkness, the air heavy with tension. Pinchas wiped the perspiration from his brow with his sleeve, licking away the beads that had formed over his upper lip. They soon heard whispers and the crunch of boots. The door creaked open. The four thieves entered stealthily, fanning out and encircling the beds. They stalked toward the immobile mounds, plunging their knives into the bedding. At that moment, Gershom fired four times in succession, motioning for the boys to follow him out of the room. They raced through the inn and out toward the stalls. The shots had alerted the innkeeper and he dashed out in his nightclothes. Before he could react, though, they were well on their way, the horses in full gallop. The night blanketing them, Gershom flicked the reins, urging the steeds to maintain a frenzied pace. Only when they were well away from the village did he allow the horses to ease into a canter, returning himself to a seated position.

"Not a pleasant experience, I'm afraid," he said evenly, letting out a deep breath.

"D...does this happen often, Poppa?" Pinchas sputtered.

Gershom laughed. "No, thank God. But, my son, if you remember to keep your eyes and ears open, you will find this can be an exciting way to earn a living," he said with a chuckle.

Pinchas laughed heartily. "Poppa, you are amazing."

"Not amazing, Pinchas," he declared, "just alert."

"I guess we'll never go back to that inn again, Poppa?"

"Well," he drawled, "I don't know. I think Ivan Feodorvich will never try that on me again. Tonight, he and his cohorts have learned a bitter lesson. In the future, his inn might just be the safest place for us," he declared.

"Are those bandits dead, Poppa?" Pinchas asked, his voice dropping.

"As I told you some time ago, one doesn't stay around long enough to find out."

Gershom then turned to Srulik. "Not the most pleasant way to bid farewell to Mother Russia, eh, my boy?"

Srulik grinned in response. "Not the most pleasant, maybe, but certainly the most unforgettable."

They travelled all that night and as the golden shafts of sunlight lifted the day from night, they could see the border ahead through the hazy morning mist.

TWELVE

YANKELEH BLINKED SEVERAL times, but still the barn rippled and undulated like waving wheat before harvest. He rubbed his eyes vigorously and tried to stretch, but his aching joints resisted movement. Worse, his head throbbed and his mouth felt parched. He suddenly wanted water more than anything else in the world.

"I think the fever broke," he heard someone whisper anxiously.

Yankeleh tried to make out the shadowy faces hovering over him. He was grateful when water was offered, and he sipped greedily. Then, exhausted from even that effort, he dropped back onto the cushion.

"How are you feeling, Yaakov?" The voice filtered through a haze.

Yankeleh wanted to reply, but no sound emerged.

"Shh, it's all right. You are fine now," the voice reassured.

"What happened?" he finally managed to mutter.

"Shh. Don't try to talk." It was Katia's voice. Her cool hand now rested on his brow. "You are fine now. Nothing to worry about."

"W…was I sick?" he asked hoarsely.

She chuckled. "Yes, I would say so, my boy."

"How…how long?" he stammered.

"Over a month," she replied. "Do you remember Vlad coming into the barn to look for you?"

"No, no, I don't remember anything, being sick, or…or anything," he said hoarsely. The image of Srulik surfaced. Yankeleh clutched the cover, his hand trembling.

"Vlad came into the barn to look for you, and he found you lying in a pool of sweat. You were talking gibberish, and your head was burning," Katia whispered. "Poor Vlad, he was beside himself with worry. We even sent for the doctor from Volodya, but he didn't know what was causing the fever. All he could do was give us some herbs, which he hoped would help. But when the fever didn't break, we sent for him again, and…" her voice quivered, "and he said he was afraid you would die. Then the rabbi from Volodya came. He had heard that you were ill, and he was terribly worried about you. But now, thank the Lord, the fever has broken," she sobbed.

"A month?" he whispered, and then his eyes closed as he fell into a deep, healing sleep. The questions were set aside for the moment.

As his strength returned, Yankeleh became aware of Katia's and Marina's devoted nursing. He was more than grateful to them, for he knew that without their care, he would not have survived. Over the weeks of convalescence, he had time to think about Srulik. He became obsessed with worry that in his delirium he may have revealed his secret.

One afternoon, Yankeleh tactfully brought the conversation around to his feverish rantings, and he asked Marina whether she remembered anything he said during that time. She bent forward, resting her chin on her hand, her brow creased. She then shook her head no.

"Most of the time, Yaakov, you muttered in your own language," she replied, "and I couldn't understand. But there were times when you looked up at me and…"

Yankeleh cut in, his pulse racing. "And what?" he asked, unable to mask his anxiety.

"Well," she drawled, "it's not really important; it's just that it was strange."

"What was strange?"

"Well, you kept calling me Miriam," she said with a faint, curious smile. "Is Miriam your sister?" she asked.

Yankeleh heaved a sigh of relief. "No, I have no sisters. I am an only child," he said quietly. And then, searching for an explanation, he added, "I guess I must have confused you with my cousin Miriam. You see, you remind me of her."

"But you never spoke of a cousin that looks like me," she said, looking puzzled.

"Well," he answered, clearing his throat, "it was hard for me to talk about my family."

"Of course," Marina replied, nodding in understanding. "I often think of how terrible it must be for you to have been taken away from your parents. I only wish there were a way for you to return to your own people," she said, shaking her head from side to side, her eyes filled with compassion.

Yankeleh flushed at her words. It was as if she had thrust an arrow into his heart. "If only you, too, could return to your people!" he thought, biting back the words.

Marina looked bewildered. "You look so sad, Yaakov. Have I said anything to upset you?"

Yankeleh swallowed hard. "It's just that it's painful for me to think about my parents, and to know that I may never see them again."

"Why is the Czar so cruel?" she demanded, unable to hide her bitterness. "And yet we worship him as if he were a god." She threw her head back, her eyes filled with contempt. "I think he is a demon, a monster," she exclaimed angrily.

Before taking her leave, she turned unexpectedly and stared at Yankeleh, her expression pained. "Yaakov, I didn't know whether to tell you or not, but now I think you should know. You see, on the very day that we found you ill, a conscript from a nearby village ran away. The police and army have been hunting for him ever since. They went to every house, even to ours, and they tried to shake you awake, to get you to talk," she said with a shiver, "but all they got was ranting in your language. So they gave up and left."

The blood drained from Yankeleh's face. "Did they ever find him?" he asked nervously.

Marina smiled. "No, not yet." And then a frown surfaced again. "But they keep looking, Yaakov. I just pray they never come here again. They were terrible, horrible people," she gasped. "And the truth is, I hope they never find him. With all of my heart I hope he gets away."

"I do, too," Yankeleh muttered under his breath.

When Marina returned with his evening meal, she seemed eager to talk. "Yaakov," she began shyly, "you have been part of our family for a long time, and yet, in all of the time that you've been with us, you have never spoken about yourself or your family. I know how painful it is, but I would like to know more about you."

Yankeleh sank back on his pillow and closed his eyes. The image of his home and his parents rose before him. Suddenly he was gripped by nostalgia, and he, too, wanted to talk, to tell someone about his wonderful home, his gentle parents, his friends. He closed his eyes and the images emerged clear and sharp. His life story came easily from his lips. When he had finished, he was drained from the effort. Marina stared down at her lap, tears rolling down her cheeks.

"Yaakov, your parents sound so wonderful, I almost envy you. Not that my parents aren't good people, and I do love them, but…sometimes I feel an emptiness that I just can't understand. I look at myself in the mirror, and…I don't feel as if I belong here. I have this odd feeling, a memory of being somewhere else, with different people around me," she said, her voice muted. "Yaakov, I don't know why I am telling you this, but something inside me makes me feel that you understand even though you are…" she paused and cleared her throat, "even though you are a Jew."

She paused thoughtfully and clasped the hands before her. "Yaakov, you are the very first Jew I have ever met," she admitted. "Before you came here, all I knew about Jews was what I heard from others. They said terrible things, unbelievable things, like Jews are in league with the devil. Not that my Poppa and Momma ever said such things, but I heard it from others, from the children in church and from their parents. They are always cursing Jews, and…and they say that the Jews themselves are cursed. But I don't believe it, not for one minute," she said angrily. "Now that I know you, Yaakov, I think it's the gentiles who are cursed because of what they have done to God's own people!"

Yankeleh stared in open-mouthed astonishment at Marina, biting back the words, "Marina, you are Miriam, you are Miriam, and you are part of our people!" The words remained locked away in a chamber of his heart, unspoken. Instead he nodded.

When Yankeleh's health improved, he began pursuing every rumor about the runaway conscript, though he dared not return to Volodya for the present. As the months rolled by and the conscript had not been found, Yankeleh began to hope that perhaps his friend had managed to escape.

It was a month before Pesach when Vlad made the

astounding suggestion that Yankeleh spend the Pesach holiday with the rabbi of Volodya.

"But I don't know the rabbi there," he replied, his eyes wide, "though I suppose I could ask him."

Vlad laughed heartily, slapping Yankeleh on the back. "No more games with me, Yaakov. When you were sick I called in the doctor from Volodya, and I told him that it was the same boy who had come to him with the back problem. He looked at me as if I were mad. `No one came to me with back problems. And I never saw this boy before,' he said to me. So," Vlad cackled, shaking his calloused finger at Yankeleh, "so, even a simple peasant like Vlad could figure out that you probably went to Volodya to see the rabbi. You know you could have told me, Yaakov. I really wouldn't have minded."

Yankeleh flushed a deep crimson, his eyes lowered. "I…I am sorry, Vlad. It's…" he shifted his feet, "well, I wasn't sure you would let me go to see the rabbi. And…"

"Ach, it's all right," he cut in, waving his hand in the air. "You know, Yaakov, you are a very popular fellow. Not only did the rabbi come by to see you, but also Father Peter came by almost every day, until he was sent to St. Petersburg on retreat. And he made me promise to remind you that he expects you to continue studying with him as soon as he returns," he added with a hint of annoyance. "Just you remember, don't let him force you to do anything you don't want to do."

Yankeleh chuckled good-naturedly. "Don't worry, Vlad. You know by now that no one makes me do anything I don't want to do."

Vlad nodded to himself and then blurted out, "Did you know, Yaakov, that I know the rabbi from Volodya?"

Yankeleh pretended surprise.

"We met a long time ago. We had sort of a misunderstanding then. But that's all in the past and best forgotten. You know, for a rabbi, he's not a bad sort, and he really worried about you, Yaakov. On one of his visits he told me that you are the son of the Kronitzer Rebbe," he said, stabbing Yankeleh in the ribs with his elbow. "So now I know that I have a very special farm hand working for me, a farm hand who also knows how to keep a secret."

Yankeleh stared at the ground. "I…I didn't think you knew anything about rebbes."

"I know what a rebbe is," Vlad exclaimed. "They are holy men, and some, I hear, can even perform miracles," he added, proud of his knowledge. "I also know, Yankeleh, that one day, if the Lord wills it, you will become the Kronitzer Rebbe." He stared at Yankeleh with admiration. "When that day comes, I hope you will remember old Vlad and Katia in your prayers, Yaakov."

Yankeleh placed his hand on Vlad's arm. "I will never forget you and Katia Ivanova," he said sincerely. "But I don't know whether the Czar will ever allow me to return to my home and my family."

When he had recuperated, Yankeleh returned to his chores and to his study sessions with Peter, who welcomed him back with a bear hug and tears. "I missed you, my boy. For a while there I really thought we had lost you. I pleaded with God, I begged Him to give you life, and I even made all kinds of deals with Him. I said, save my friend and I will be a better man, and a more diligent student. So now I have no choice but to study harder," he said with a warm chuckle.

Restored to health, with his friend Srulik far away from danger, Yankeleh enjoyed a brief taste of contentment. But his happiness soon came to an end. It was a week before Pesach when he overheard a conversation that chilled his blood.

"Can you believe our luck, Katia? Yuri Ustyag says his son Boris wants to marry our Marina!" Vlad exclaimed with glee. "He told me that he didn't care that we can't give her a dowry, and for the sake of Boris's happiness, he is even willing to give us five acres of good farmland, if we agree," Vlad Stepanovich declared, his eyes bright with expectation.

Katia sneered. "Boris is nothing but a drunken lout. Our Marina is too good for him."

"Too good? What makes her too good?" he bellowed. "We have nothing and they have land, Katia. And now, at last, we'll have land, too."

"Ach, you're blind. All you see is land, land. What about our child? Have you forgotten who she is? How can you give her to that drunken pig?"

Vlad skulked off, shouting, "Do you have someone better in mind, someone with a better offer?"

"There will be someone better," she shrieked.

"I'm not giving up good land, old woman, do you hear?" he growled, shaking a fist at his wife.

Yankeleh felt faint. He dropped the tools he had been carrying and raced toward the barn, where he sat on his cot and wept.

Yankeleh spent a festive Chol HaMoed Pesach at the home of Rabbi Duvid Malinsky. He felt a warm closeness to the rabbi, who had quietly accepted Yankeleh's apology for having disobeyed him. "You endangered yourself, and others, too," the rabbi had said, "but God has been merciful, and no one was harmed." A fair man, he added, "perhaps I, too, erred, in underestimating the danger your friend was in. Thank God he is safe."

Yankeleh was particularly grateful to Rabbi Malinsky for serving as intermediary between him and his parents. He was now able to correspond with them freely, though the joy of the exchange of letters was tempered by the knowledge that his parents had been warned not to visit Volodya for fear that their visit might endanger him. Yankeleh accepted this reality with anguished stoicism, grateful at least for their letters, which nourished his soul. They also sent him, despite his objections, a sizeable sum of money, insisting that one never knew when the money might be useful.

"Don't spend it on frivolous things, even if tempted," Rabbi Malinsky cautioned. "No one must ever know that you have rubles. It could be dangerous for you. Remember to be prudent," he warned.

Following the rabbi's advice, Yankeleh hid the

money in a hole he had dug under his bed in the barn.

In the course of his visit, Yankeleh raised a subject that had been preying on his mind. "Rabbi Malinsky, I am very troubled," he said, his eyes reflecting his anxiety. He then repeated the conversation he had overheard between Katia and Vlad.

The rabbi sat hunched over, his head in his hands.

"Rabbi, we must prevent such a terrible tragedy from taking place."

To Yankeleh's relief, the rabbi nodded his head in agreement. "Yes, yes, we must," he said quietly. "It's not as if I did not anticipate such an eventuality, but to my mind, Miriam is still a child," he muttered as he stroked his beard. "How old can she be? Almost sixteen? She is a child, and yet not a child," he sighed. "I must give this some thought, Yaakov.

"This is a very delicate matter. Again, I beg you, do not interfere. You are not to say anything to Marina or her parents. On this I am adamant. All I ask of you is to keep your eyes and ears open. If Vlad continues his negotiations with Yuri Ustyag, let me know of their progress. And that is all you are to do for the moment."

Over the next few months, Yankeleh used every ruse he could think of, short of asking outright, to find out whether Yuri Ustyag's proposal of a match between Boris and Marina was being considered seriously by Vlad. For the moment, however, Vlad focused all of his energies on the spring planting. This was followed by summer and the fall harvest. Yankeleh had long fallen into the rhythm of the land, which left little time for leisurely speculation

about the future. For the time being, there were no signs
of further negotiations with Yuri Ustyag.

There was one bright exception to the drudgery of
work in Yankeleh's life. Not even exhaustion could keep
Yankeleh from his twice-weekly study sessions with Father
Peter Fyodorovich Kuskov. These sessions continued to
disturb Vlad, who assumed that the priest still had ulterior
motives. There were times when Yankeleh was tempted to
put Vlad's mind at ease about Peter's intentions, but both
he and Peter agreed that it was safer for Vlad to think that
he was still studying for baptism. The stimulating hours
spent with Peter honed Yankeleh's intellectual skills. Deep
in his heart, he hoped that his hours of study would help,
in part, to make up for the life that he had been forced to
lead away from his people.

With the cycle of sowing and harvesting coming to
an end, preparations were again in earnest for the annual
fall fair. Just days before the fair, Vlad stomped into the
barn to examine his favorite steed. With a practiced eye,
he checked the horse's hoofs and legs.

"Ach," Vlad exclaimed, shaking his head sadly, "he
won't make it through another winter. I have no choice,
I have to sell him. It's the only way I can scrape together
enough money to buy another horse. This old fellow is
worn out," he muttered sadly, stroking the horse's flanks.

Yankeleh rubbed the old horse behind the ear as he
listened to Vlad's bitter assessment of the animal's future.
Pangs of guilt assailed him when he remembered how
hard he had ridden the old horse, how he had bravely

responded to Yankeleh's frantic demands and brought him home safely. It wasn't fair, he thought with a grimace. The old horse had given his all, and now, instead of enjoying old age with plenty of fodder, he was to be sold and probably slaughtered for glue.

"Isn't there another way to raise the money, Vlad?" Yankeleh entreated.

Vlad shook his head. "Na, no way, Yaakov. And even if I do sell him, I'm not so sure that I'll have enough."

Yankeleh leaned his head on the old horse's flank. "There's got to be another way, Vlad."

Vlad patted Yankeleh's shoulder. "You're a good lad, Yaakov. I know how you feel, but that's life," he exclaimed, throwing his hands in the air.

That night, Yankeleh brooded over the situation. There just had to be a way to save the horse. When he had almost despaired of a solution, the answer came. Yankeleh almost laughed out loud, the answer had been so obvious.

They had loaded the last basket onto the wagon and, with exhausted sighs, now stared at the rich harvest readied for market. It had been a good year, and the crops were abundant and succulent.

"What'll I do without you when the army takes you away?" Vlad observed, clapping Yankeleh on the shoulder. "You've turned into a good farmer," he said with pride.

"That's because I have a good teacher," Yankeleh replied with a glint in his eye. "But we still have two more years together."

When his three sons had trudged back to the cottage, Vlad unexpectedly turned to Yankeleh and, with an emotional depth that astounded him, said, "You're a fine lad, a fine lad, Yaakov."

"I know it's hard to believe," Yankeleh replied with a playful grin, "but you're a good fellow too, Vlad."

"Naw," he said, scratching behind his ear, "I'm just a dumb peasant."

"You're not dumb, Vlad. You're a good farmer, and you do your best for your family," he said, turning serious. "Believe me, knowing how to read and write doesn't make a man smart. It takes more than that, and I know." And then with a chuckle, he continued. "Remember yesterday when you talked about selling the horse? And this smart fellow here," he said, pointing to himself, "was ready to let you sell your old workhorse, because with all my smartness I wasn't thinking."

"What're you ranting about, Yaakov? The fever got you again?" Vlad said with a worried expression.

"No, no fever this time, Vlad. Listen carefully. I have some money, money my parents gave to me. Don't ask me how I managed to get it, it's not important," he said, not wanting to reveal the current correspondence with his parents, "but I think I have enough to buy a young stallion."

Vlad gaped at Yankeleh. "I can't take your money, lad. You'll need it later. Who knows what the future holds for you?"

"I beg you, Vlad. Please. Take the money. Only promise me that you won't sell the old horse."

Vlad threw his arms about Yankeleh, his eyes moist.

An icy wind blew hard as they arrived at the fairground. Still, the air crackled with excitement, the flags fluttered, the vendors shouted their wares, and the children raced to and fro, enjoying their infrequent treats. At Yankeleh's insistence, Vlad had accepted the money for the horse, and thanks to his shrewd bargaining ability, he managed to purchase two horses instead of one: a handsome, bay Belgium draft horse to pull the plow and haul heavy loads, and a frisky, sure-footed one-year-old quarter horse for riding and other farm chores. Vlad slapped Yankeleh on the back with satisfaction at the conclusion of the negotiations, ignoring the sullen peasants ogling them.

With a brisk step, Yankeleh then headed toward the section of the Jewish artisans, hoping to find Lazar Farbstein again, and perhaps learn about the fate of his friend Srulik. As he was making his way through the crowd, he heard Marina's voice rising above the clamor. Something made him turn. He saw Marina a short distance away, with Yuri Ustyag's son Boris standing next to her, trying to embrace her by force. Yankeleh rushed to Marina's side. Breathless, he shouted, "Why don't you leave her alone!"

"Mind your own business, yid," Boris grunted, turning again to Marina. "Come on, don't be so uppity with me. My father will soon fix it up so that you'll be mine for keeps, and then we'll see about your airs," he threatened, as she pushed him away.

Yankeleh's pulse raced. "Get your hands off her!" he shouted, glaring at Boris.

His face bright red, Boris pounced on him. Yankeleh tried unsuccessfully to shield himself from the shower of blows. But when the raucous, jeering crowd started closing in on him, Yankeleh was stirred to the offensive, and he began to return the blows with a sure aim. An ominous hush alerted him. Yankeleh flinched and drew back—the thrust of Boris's knife missed him by inches. Marina screamed. Yankeleh lunged forward, and he grabbed Boris's hand, twisting it with force, until he wrenched the knife from his grasp. Panting from the effort, he still managed to knock Boris to the ground. Yankeleh snatched up the knife, which lay near his opponent's grasp, and shoved it into his boot. He then trudged off, a trembling though grateful Marina at his side.

On their way home, Yankeleh, seated next to Vlad on the wagon, recounted the details of the fight, not hiding his pride in his victory. Vlad sat hunched over, tugging the harness as he encouraged the team to a more energetic gait. He stared ahead, not commenting as Yankeleh continued with growing animation. Without turning his head, Vlad muttered, "You still got Boris's knife?"

Yankeleh started. He pulled the knife from his boot and then, with distaste, threw it across the road into a thicket. "That's the last I want to see of it," Yankeleh cried.

"You were foolish to interfere," Vlad muttered, his tone harsh. "You won this round, but you're no match for him and his friends. They'll be out looking for you," he warned.

"But he was badgering Marina!"

"Marina is old enough to take care of herself. And if she needs help, she has her father and brothers," Vlad growled.

Yankeleh glanced sidelong at Vlad. He knew only too well what triggered Vlad's anger, and he fought hard to contain his own.

"From now on, be on your guard," Vlad hissed, his eyes fixed on the road.

For some inexplicable reason, Yankeleh looked back at the thicket where he had thrown Boris's knife. Yankeleh trembled, gripped by a sudden sense of foreboding.

THIRTEEN

YANKELEH TRUDGED THROUGH the snow, exhaling huge clouds of vapor. He hunched forward, his eyes smarting with tears of cold. More than anything else, he wanted to be alone. He thrust his hands into his pockets and stared up at the huge, white-hooded conifers. The fresh, mid-day air cleared his head, and the tranquility of the forest soothed him, stilling his anxiety. He blinked at the bright sunlight, and thought about Marina.

It had been a bitter winter. Blizzards had battered the Ruszkys' flimsy cottage and barn without mercy. When the weather finally broke, Yankeleh borrowed Vlad's sleigh and made his way to Volodya, a grueling journey in the best of times. But he dared not delay.

Breathless, his body numb from the bracing cold, he sank into a chair opposite Rabbi Malinsky. With painful detail, he related the events of the past few months. His voice wavered when he described the crucial visit. "Boris's father came just days before the snow made roads totally impassable," he began. "And when he left, they shook hands as if they had arrived at an understanding. They were together for a long time. I could see them drinking and talking through the window, but could only hear an occasional word or two. At one point Katia shouted, and then I knew that things were not going well. The next day Katia spoke to no one—she seemed agitated, very nervous. Marina, too, said little, and her eyes were red-rimmed. I am certain they have agreed to the match. We may be too late."

Rabbi Malinsky rubbed his hand over his eyes, and his shoulders sagged wearily. "Yaakov, I won't deceive you. What you have just related is indeed serious. You are right, Vlad Stepanovich has probably come to some understanding with the boy's father." He paused, and cleared his throat. "We will have to act quickly, before it's too late. The promise of five acres of land has blinded Vlad Stepanovich. He is committing Marina to a life of misery. And it is our Miriam, a Jewish child, who is the *kaparah* in this arrangement." He closed his eyes in thought. "We will have to find a way. We will have to find something to entice him if we are to prevent this heinous match from taking place."

Yankeleh's eyes remained fixed on the rabbi, his heart sinking with each word.

"Our problem, Yaakov, is that land is not easy to come by. Even with a great deal of money, it isn't a simple matter to coax someone into selling his farmland. But it must be done," he said with growing urgency. "It must be done. Tomorrow, I will meet with the leaders of the *kahal,* and we will map out a plan. That much I can assure you."

"But how can you get land?" Yankeleh asked tremulously.

Rabbi Malinsky spoke in measured tones. Stroking his beard, he considered the problem. "There just may be an answer," he murmered, his eyes glimmering with a spark of hope. "It is known that a childless widow, Ekatarina Kartaly, owns a farm not far from the Ruszkys', and she leases some of her land in return for a portion of the yield. Perhaps we can convince her to sell some of her land, or perhaps she would agree to a long-term lease. This is one possible solution," he muttered, almost to himself.

"Do you think she would agree?" Yankeleh gushed eagerly, his eyes wide with hope.

The rabbi shrugged. "Let's just say that it offers a possibility. In the meantime, you must continue to keep us informed of any new developments. I have a feeling that Vlad Stepanovich would want to take title to the land before the spring planting."

Yankeleh sat stunned for a few moments. He leaned over and gripped the edge of the table. "So soon?"

"My son, if I judge that peasant correctly, he is not really so eager to give his favorite daughter to the loutish son of Yuri Ustyag. And from the way you describe Katia Ivanova and Marina's feelings, another solution would be more than welcome." Rabbi Malinksy rubbed his brow. "Something tells me that Katia Ivanova's conscience troubles her, and we must use her conscience as leverage to save Marina and bring her back to her people."

"Rabbi, we must tell Marina that she is Jewish," Yankeleh blurted out, his heart beating rapidly.

Rabbi Malinsky observed Yankeleh and then nodded thoughtfully.

"Yes, Yaakov, the time is fast approaching for Marina to learn the truth about her heritage. But," he said, heaving a sigh, "you see, Yaakov, even after she learns about her parentage, we cannot force her to return to us. The decision will ultimately be hers. Of course you realize that Marina, or Miriam, has no memory of her parents or her past. We can only hope that when she learns who she is, she will make the right choice. For the present, our priority is to prevent the marriage. And then we will pray for *HaKadosh Baruch Hu* to show her the right path."

Yankeleh sank back into the chair, engulfed by doubts. "But she must return to her people, she must!"

Rabbi Malinsky observed Yankeleh silently for a moment, a small smile emerging.

"Let us pray that she does, Yaakov," he replied gently. "But now, my dear Yaakov, there is another hurdle to overcome. If, despite our offer, Vlad Stepanovich still insists on going ahead with the match, then we will have a serious problem to contend with."

"Vlad would never do that!" Yankeleh exclaimed.

"I know that Vlad is not an evil man, Yaakov. But land is a great temptation, and, if he feels that Yuri Ustyag's offer is better, well, who knows how he will react to our interference? Yaakov, by now you should know what land means to a farmer, and Vlad is a hungry, landless farmer. He might think that we are trying to take this rare opportunity away from him, and to make matters worse, we also plan to take his daughter away from him. We must not forget that, no matter how we feel, Vlad and Katia have come to think of Marina as their very own daughter."

Yankeleh could not suppress a groan.

Rabbi Malinsky shifted closer, his voice hoarse. "But be assured, Yaakov, I will move heaven and earth to prevent this marriage. But first things first. We must make Vlad Stepanovich an offer he will find hard to refuse. And then, Yaakov, no matter whether he accepts the offer or not, Marina will be told of her heritage. With God's help, she will return to us. My rebbetzin is ready to take Miriam into our home. She will instruct her and prepare her to return to her people as a good Jewish daughter, if God wills it. But for the present, I beg you, Yaakov, be cautious. Do not take things into your own hands. This matter is extremely delicate. Any word to Marina now could endanger everything," he said. "Now we must both pray that the *Ribono Shel Olam* will guide our steps."

Spring burst upon them with a gush of rainstorms that left the land corrugated in mud. After weeks of incessant rain, on an almost cloudless day, a fine coach, drawn by four matched mahogany-colored steeds, clattered to a halt in front of the Ruszky cottage. Five distinguished men alighted, greeting an astonished Vlad Stepanovich with smiles and handshakes. They were immediately ushered into the cottage. Yankeleh hung back in the shadows, not eager for these fine-looking Jews to see him. Too nervous to do his chores, he waited anxiously for the visit to end. The minutes ticked by, and two hours later, they finally emerged. Yankeleh was covered with sweat, his body aching from tension. The members of the *kahal* shook hands with Vlad, their eyes expressionless. Yankeleh shivered. Though Vlad could not fail but appreciate Yankeleh's interest in such a rare visit, he remained silent. Nor did Katia's expression enlighten him.

On the following day, Yankeleh helped Vlad shore up the rain-weakened fences. Vlad stopped to catch his breath, and mopping his brow, he exclaimed, "I feel in my bones that this will be a good year," he said, his grin revealing blunt, rotted teeth. "The early spring will give us a good start. And besides," he chortled, "I have had some unexpectedly good offers."

Yankeleh blanched, trying to conceal the tremble in his voice. "Good offers?"

"Yeh! You wouldn't believe it, Yaakov. Suddenly, everyone loves old Vlad," he laughed. "I got a lot to think about, a lot to think about," he said, scratching his head.

"Is there anything I can help you with?" Yankeleh inquired with mock innocence.

"You?" he yelped, clapping his calloused hand on Yankeleh's shoulder. "Nah," he chuckled.

Yankeleh's throat was tight as he returned to work. He scanned the short distance between himself and Vlad. What was old Vlad thinking? he wondered. He took a deep breath and continued pounding the wooden stake into the ground, whispering a brief prayer.

✶   ✶   ✶

Yankeleh was startled out of his sleep by a crescendo of sound. He lifted himself on one elbow, staring at the barn door. Was he dreaming or did he actually hear pounding? He shook his head to try and clear it. Again he heard the pounding. It was not a dream. Alarmed, Yankeleh sat bolt upright. He heard shouts, Vlad cursing loudly, and then wailing. The sound of boots smacking against viscous mud grew louder. Yankeleh leaped from his cot and dressed quickly. The barn door crashed open. Six men, dressed in the uniforms of the local gendarmerie, stood before him, their hands on their weapons.

In the shadowy light of the lantern Yankeleh saw Vlad's face distorted with terror, and Katia Ivanova, next to him, wringing her hands.

"Are you the conscript Yaakov Yitzchak Halevi?" the officer in charge barked.

"Yes," Yankeleh said, his voice quivering.

"Get your coat and shoes and come with us," the man ordered, shoving Yankeleh roughly.

"Why? What have I done?"

The officer cuffed Yankeleh behind the ear. "You'll find out soon enough, that is, if you don't already know, yid," he sneered.

Yankeleh instinctively drew away. "What do you want? I haven't done anything. What's happening, Vlad?" he pleaded, looking toward Vlad for help.

"Yaakov, it's a mistake. I told them. Just go along and

everything will be straightened out by morning."

"But Vlad, what do they want?"

"Get your shoes on, yid, and move," the officer ordered, striking Yankeleh with greater force.

Yankeleh's eyes met Vlad's panic-filled gaze as he was dragged into the black night.

Hours later, he found himself in the gray, forbidding prison in Kirov. His hands and feet were manacled, and he was thrown into a dank cell. The sliver of moonlight provided Yankeleh with enough light to see a straw pallet on the filthy, straw-covered floor. He sank down, bewildered, waiting for dawn to break. At last Yankeleh could see the patches of somber sky from the tiny, barred window in the ceiling. Much later, two police guards opened the cell door and, without a word, pulled him to his feet. They dragged his manacled body into a room with grime-covered walls. Forced to attention, Yankeleh noticed for the first time the glaring eyes of Yuri Ustyag, the father of Boris.

"He's the one. He took my son's knife. As God is my witness, he murdered him," he shrieked, straining toward Yankeleh, ready to pounce. Restrained by the warders, his face ballooned into a red rage.

Yankeleh stood motionless. The word "No!," exploded from the deepest recesses of his soul.

"He's the one, he killed my Boris. That Jew murdered my boy!" Yuri Ustyag screeched.

His wife, standing behind him, pointed her gnarled finger at Yankeleh, her face contorted in hate. "That Jew killed him. He's the one who took his knife. I saw him, I saw him with my own eyes," she howled.

Yankeleh was shoved back to his cell. As the door clanged shut, the warder glared malevolently and spat at him. "Filthy scum. Murderer," he grunted. "You'll get yours, you'll feel the rope around your yid neck soon."

Yankeleh fell to the ground, mute, his eyes staring at the blank wall before him. Slowly, very slowly, the tears formed and ran down his face, catching in his just emerging beard. He could still hear the woman's moans and shouts, "Murderer, murderer!" Yankeleh shuddered. What was happening to him? He sat unmoving, not touching the bowl of cabbage soup at his side, not even noticing the family of rats scampering about, greedily feasting on the soup. It couldn't be happening to him. It was a nightmare, but he would soon awaken and it would be over.

The days passed and the nightmare refused to evaporate. No one came, not Vlad, not Katia, not Peter, not the rabbi. No one. He refused to eat the soup, drinking only the foul-tasting water and eating the dry bread. Outside of the surly warder who threw in the slops and spat at him whenever he passed the steel cell door, there were only the rats for companionship. He sat immobilized, waiting, and not knowing what he was waiting for or what awaited him.

He tried to keep track of time by observing the sliver of sky from the narrow, barred window, spacing his prayers in accordance with the shadows that indicated morning, noon, and night. Four days went by in a nightmarish dream, until the warder waddled into his cell and dragged the fast-weakened Yankeleh to his feet, pushing and kicking him toward a room with a cauldron of heated water.

"Wash yourself, you filthy yid," the warder growled, holding his nose in disgust.

Yankeleh followed the man's orders eagerly, and then pulled on the clean, though rough, prison uniform. Again manacled, he was led through a maze of corridors and locked doors until he stumbled into a moldy, windowless room. It was bare, except for a table and two chairs. Resting on the table were sheafs of paper, writing implements, several seals, and a huge leather briefcase. A large man with a red face glared at him from behind the table, his bulbous nose perched atop a thick mustache. An unkempt thatch of black hair hung over his ears, and his thick, hairy fingers drummed impatiently on the table before him. He looked at Yankeleh from under eyebrows that met in the middle, his steely blue eyes appraising him. He indicated for Yankeleh to be seated.

"What is your full name?" he barked in a voice as gruff as his appearance.

Yankeleh swallowed hard. His mouth dry, he tried to form his words. "Halevi, Yaakov Yitzchak."

The man wrote slowly and carefully.

"Where are you from?"

"Kronitz Podolsk, sir."

"Do you know the charge against you?"

Yankeleh shook his head. "Not formally, sir."

"Hmm," he hummed, a tight grin surfacing, "a clever

one, too. Very well, Yaakov Yitzchak Halevi. Now that you've introduced yourself to me," he said with a cynical chuckle, "it is my turn to introduce myself to you. I am Serge Mikhailovich Noujik, the investigating magistrate of your case. Do you understand what that means? You have been charged with murder. The charge will now be investigated and then presented to the District Court, where it will be confirmed or disapproved. Only when confirmed will you have the right to counsel, that is, to engage a lawyer. Is that clear, Yaakov Yitzchak Halevi?" he sneered.

Yankeleh shook his head yes.

The investigating magistrate rose, drawing his fingers through his flourishing mustache. He turned to Yankeleh, his legs apart, his eyes hard and glowering. "You have been charged with the murder of Boris Ustyag. How do you plead?"

"I am not guilty, sir. I have never harmed anyone, sir. As God is my witness, I am innocent, sir."

"Do you deny initiating a fist fight with Boris Ustyag at the fall county fair?"

"We fought," he said evenly, "but I did not start the fight."

"No matter," he exclaimed with an impatient flick of his hand. "Why did you fight with Boris Ustyag?"

Yankeleh passed a hand across his face. He knew only too well the meaning of self-incrimination. He had to be cautious.

"Boris Ustyag was trying to…to force his attentions on Marina, Marina Ruszky, the daughter of my master. I merely asked him to refrain, and he attacked me."

"And, young man, who gave you the right to interfere in a simple flirtation?"

The words struck Yankeleh like a slap. He wiped the sweat from his brow with his sleeve and tried to avoid the investigating magistrate's piercing gaze.

"I saw Marina reject his advances. She pleaded with him to leave her alone."

"I see. After the fight did you take his knife?"

"Yes. He was about to attack me with it, and I grabbed it from him."

"And what happened next? What happened to that knife?"

"On my way home I threw it in the brambles, somewhere along the road. You can ask my master, Vlad Ruszky."

"We know whom to ask," he exclaimed sharply.

Yankeleh looked down at his lap, fighting against the terror that held him in its grip. In all of his years as a cantonist, facing threats, torture, and pain, never had he felt such uncontrollable fear.

"You were jealous of Boris Ustyag, weren't you?" the magistrate sneered. "You provoked a fight, you stole the knife, and then you waited for your chance to kill him."

Yaakov felt the walls closing in on him. "It's a lie, a slanderous lie," he cried.

"So it is a lie, is it, Jew? Well, we'll see. Even the likes of you will have your day in court. Then we will see."

Once again the warder, cursing under his breath,

dragged Yankeleh through the maze of prison corridors and threw him into his cell. When the steel door slammed behind him, Yankeleh sank onto the pallet, at long last giving in to the torrent of pain that flowed from his tortured soul. The words that had been trapped within him exploded in a heart rending wail.

When he finally calmed himself, he tried to piece together his thoughts. He shuddered, closing his eyes and rocking to and fro, the tears merging with his words. "*Ribono Shel Olam*, have pity on this unworthy mortal, take pity on me. Save me, not for my own sake, *Ribono Shel Olam*, but for the sake of my father, for his father before him, and all the Halevis who have died *al kiddush Hashem*, going to their death for the sanctification of Your holy name."

In his despair Yankeleh refused to touch any food but bread and water, and he grew increasingly frail. He knew that the outcome of the trial was a foregone conclusion. Who would believe the word of a Jew, an unwanted cantonist? Besides, he realized, this was not an accusation against him alone! All the Jews of the area would suffer. The authorities were seeking an excuse for a pogrom, and these trumped-up charges would give it to them. His last communication with the investigating magistrate only confirmed his fears. The charge had been approved and the trial would be scheduled soon, the magistrate had affirmed with a terrible smile. No lawyer had appeared, no one had come to represent him. Not that it mattered, he thought. No lawyer could save him. The trap had been set, and it was only a matter of time before he would be crushed in its steel grip. He had chosen the path of starvation. He could not face a trial that would be an empty mockery of justice. Better to die first, and not give them the satisfaction of killing him.

Yankeleh was drawn from his dreary thoughts by the clang of the cell door opening. He looked up, anticipating the brutish face of his warder. Instead, his gaze met the florid, ugly face of Serge Mikhailovich Noujik, the investigating magistrate. His arms and legs shackled, Yankeleh had no need to rise to greet his unexpected guest.

"I am told, Yaakov Yitzchak Halevi, that you refuse to eat."

Yankeleh stared up at the man, uninterested.

"You have a long and arduous road ahead of you, and you need your strength."

"Why?" the word came out in a croak.

The investigating magistrate returned his stare, and exclaimed, "Why, indeed. Still, you must eat. We have arranged for you to have kosher food."

Yankeleh gaped at the investigating magistrate in disbelief. "What does it matter whether I eat or not, sir? The verdict is already in. I am condemned. My people are condemned," he said bitterly.

"You will have every opportunity to defend yourself, Yaakov Yitzchak Halevi, in a court of law," he said with a touch of irritation. "Just have patience. Now I suggest, young man, that you begin eating. I will order the warder to see that these shackles are removed, that you bathe regularly, and get clean clothes. We are a civilized nation, young man, and you are indeed fortunate to be in this enlightened prison."

Yankeleh swallowed the spittle that filled his mouth, and barely suppressed his rage.

The following day, Yankeleh watched with disbelief as an elderly Jew with a long, white beard, carrying a basket, followed the warder into his cell.

"Yaakov Yitzchak," the old man began in Yiddish, "I am Reb Nachman Sokolov, a simple man, a tailor by profession. Now I ask you for your forbearance, I ask you to listen to this simple man. Though our community in Kirov is small, we are united behind you, my son. If you could hear our prayers, you would know how much we care, how great is our desire to rescue you from this fire. Since your arrest, there has been no rest for any of us.

"You can imagine my shock when a member of the police came to my home yesterday. And if his visit was a shock, his manner was even more surprising. You see, he was very polite…yes, I would even say apologetic. He said that he knew a visit from the police was always frightening, and so he was sorry if he upset us in any way. He added that he came to us on an errand of mercy. He then told us about you, as if we did not already know, and he asked my wife if she would be willing to cook meals for you, and of course they would pay for the expense. He said the police had made inquiries and knew that I was a pious man and respected in the community. He explained that you were the son of an important holy man, and you would not eat their prison fare. I wanted to say to him, 'Who in his right mind would want to eat prison fare?' but instead I listened attentively and held my peace. Before he could even finish speaking, my wife had agreed."

Yankeleh looked into the eyes of this gentle man, and his chest tightened. "Reb Nachman, what good is food to a dying man? Why should I nourish my body when my soul will soon join its Maker? I have no need for sustenance, but I thank you and your wife for your kindness."

With effort, the elderly man crouched down beside Yankeleh. His voice muted, he spoke in a guarded whisper. "My son, don't think we don't know what is in your heart and how you must suffer. But don't let them destroy you. Don't let them make you commit a mortal sin. I beg you with all of my heart, eat, become strong. In the end you will have accomplished nothing by your fast. You will be carried into court a pitiable skeleton for everyone to snicker at. *Chalilah* that you should die by your own hand. Have you so little faith in your Father in heaven?" He bent over and kissed the top of Yankeleh's bowed head. "Be brave, my son, be strong and of good courage. The Lord will be with you," he whispered hoarsely.

Before Yankeleh could reply, both Reb Nachman Sokolov and the warder were gone. Yankeleh was ready to spurn the food, when the aroma drew him to the basket. He rubbed his now unshackled wrists and peered inside. The sight of the roasted chicken, the pieces of gefilte fish, and the huge chunk of kugel, combined with Reb Nachman Sokolov's encouraging words, weakened his resolve not to eat, and Yankeleh tasted his first morsel of food in almost two weeks.

The days passed in monotonous order. He would awaken, wash, recite his morning prayers, and wait for the

clang of the warder's keys, which announced the first meal
of the day. For some reason he was being ignored. One
day slid into another without the sound of another human
voice. Why was he being kept in solitary confinement,
incommunicado? The investigating magistrate had
hinted broadly that he had been abandoned, forsaken by
the Ruszkys, by the Jewish community of Volodya, by his
parents. Forsaken, forgotten. It smarted at first and then
began to eat at his soul. And then, one morning, after
reciting his prayers, the truth rose before him, clear and
sharp.

Why hadn't he seen it before? How had they clouded
his mind? They were toying with him. It was all a game,
a sham. He had almost forgotten the supportive words
of Reb Nachman. He now realized that this was all part
of the dehumanizing process. He was being allowed to
build his own hell, one worse than the existing hell of
prison. They thought they could demoralize him, destroy
him by weakening his resolve. But he was not going to
make it easy for them.

Now that he understood their strategy and
recognized their motives, his loneliness turned into a
blessing, for the longer Yankeleh was left alone to think,
the clearer everything became. Though imprisoned, his
spirit remained free. He could reach out to God and
be succored by His presence, a presence he felt more
intensely now than at any other time in his life. Reb
Nachman had been right, and the food prepared for him
by Reb Nachman's good wife gave him the sustenance he
needed to prevail against the forces of evil massed against
him. He was ready to do battle, and he would not fail. He

would not waver from his mission.

He rehearsed the words he would shout in court, words that would crush the vicious lies being perpetrated against him. Surely the authorities realized that he had nothing to do with Boris' death. They had simply seen this as a means of further degrading the Jews, once again giving the peasantry someone to hate—so that their hatred would not turn upon their true oppressors, the ruling classes. Czar Nicholas and his predecessors were nothing more than murderous autocrats ruling over millions of Russians whom they kept chained to poverty and misery, using the Jew as their expendable safety valve against revolution. It was easy to ignite a pogrom—the murder of a Christian by a Jew would do as a pretext. The peasants and workers needed their scapegoat, and the spilling of Jewish blood relieved frustrations. He closed his eyes, and the image of the Czar's Cossacks rose before him, racing through towns and villages, their sabers drawn, using Jewish children for target practice. He groaned and bile filled his mouth. Once again he called upon the *Ribono Shel Olam*, this time for courage. He could not give up, he must not, he dare not.

FOURTEEN

FATHER PETER KUSKOV groped for his robe and stumbled toward the front door. The grandfather clock had just chimed 3:00 a.m. The pounding on the door grew increasingly urgent. He peered through the window and in the flickering light of the oil lamp, he saw the shadowed figure of Katia Ivanova, her head swaddled in a black shawl, weeping uncontrollably. He opened the door quickly and beckoned her in, his heart beating like a sledgehammer in his ears.

"Katia Ivanova, I beg you, tell me what has happened!" he beseeched, unable to elicit an intelligible word from the hysterical woman.

She continued to moan, covering her face with her work-worn hands. At last she managed to sputter, "It's Yaakov…the police…they took him, they took Yaakov."

Peter steadied himself against a chair. "But…but what do they want with him?" he stammered.

"God help us," she wailed. "Boris Ustyag is dead, and they say he killed him."

He pressed his palms against his eyes and muffled a cry of anguish. "Dead? Boris Ustyag dead? But what has this to do with Yaakov? He wouldn't harm a fly."

"I know, I know," she cried. "Vlad and I tried to tell them, but they wouldn't listen. They just dragged him away," she whimpered, mopping the tears still streaming down her face, "like a common criminal."

"Do you know where they took him?"

"To the Litansky Prison in Kirov," she sobbed.

He took Katia Ivanova's trembling hand in his own, searching for words of reassurance and comfort, words he sorely needed himself.

"Stay here until morning, Katia Ivanova," he suggested, leading her to a chair. "I will ride out to Kirov at dawn and try to sort things out. I am sure we will get to the bottom of this. It is just a dreadful mistake. Now try to calm yourself."

"We must do something, we must!" she pleaded. "You know the police, they hate Jews. They will kill him, I know it," she cried out. "We must do something!"

Tears rimmed Father Peter's eyes. "Katia Ivanova, you are a good and generous woman," he sighed, patting her shoulder. "For the present, all we can do is to pray that the good Lord will not forsake our friend Yaakov. Come, Katia Ivanova, join me in chapel and let us pray together for him."

At the brink of dawn, Father Peter saddled his

horse and raced off to Kirov, arriving at the gates of the infamous Litansky Prison in the full of morning, his body damp from sweat and the thin, nonstop drizzle.

His clerical clothing gained him immediate entrance, and he was directed to the prison reception hall, a cold, cavernous room, almost bare of furnishings. A number of grizzled warders milled about, joking, wrangling, and drinking. A middle-aged warder dressed in a rumpled uniform was seated behind a worm-eaten table. Between sips of tea, he eyed Father Peter with casual curiosity.

"What brings the good Father out on this miserable spring day?" he inquired affably. "Visiting one of your sinners?" he added with a broad wink.

Father Peter returned a tight, unfelt grin. "Indeed, not a sinner," he said with a friendly nod. "You have arrested a student of mine, a good, honest lad. His name is Yaakov Halevi."

The murmurings stopped. All eyes now focused on Father Peter as the room became deathly quiet. The ranking warder eyed the priest suspiciously as he scratched his scruffy beard. "The Jew? Your student?" he repeated with a skeptical grunt.

Father Peter Kuskov nodded affirmatively. He cleared his throat. "My student is studying for baptism," he affirmed, aware that discretion was the better part of valor.

The room filled with chortling, breaking the heavy silence.

"Yeh? Wants to become a good Christian after what he did?"

"What's the charge?" Peter asked, pretending ignorance.

The warder stared at him coldly. "The Jew murdered a good Christian, Father."

"Murder? Yaakov Halevi a murderer? That can't be!" he exploded. "I know the lad. He wouldn't harm a fly. Has he confessed to such a heinous crime?"

"Confess? Not yet. But he will."

"Listen, I think there has been a terrible mistake. Let me see him. I am sure I can ferret out the truth. He trusts me. I might even save the police a lot of trouble," he suggested a shade too eagerly.

The warder's face darkened and he shook his head. "No one can see him, no one. Sorry, those are my orders, Father."

"Then can I see the investigating magistrate?"

"Sorry. That's not possible. He'll be in St. Petersburg for the next few days."

"Isn't there anyone in charge with whom I can talk?"

The warder shrugged and smiled, pointing to the insignia that marked his rank. "Only me."

"Then can't you make an exception? I am a priest. What harm can come from my visit?"

"Sorry, strict orders—no one," he said sullenly.

"All right then, when can I see him?" he said, clearly exasperated.

The police officer spread his hands before him and once again shrugged. "Not for a long time, Father. And if you want some good advice, don't waste your time on him. He's a bad one." His eyes narrowed. "They are evil, these Jews, and now one of them has murdered a good Christian. But the Russian people will see justice done, to him and to his cursed people."

A slow shudder gripped Father Peter. He thanked the police officer and rushed out of the prison. Gusts of cold wind and rain whipped his cassock about him, but he ignored them. There was no time to lose. He had to get to Volodya that very day.

By the time he arrived, the foul weather had dissipated. Exhausted, he dismounted to water and feed his sweating, snorting horse. He then picked his way through the maze of narrow streets in search of Rabbi Malinsky's home, which Yaakov had once described as located near the main synagogue. He finally stopped before a majestic brick building with a menorah chiseled over the entrance. There were two modest cottages on both sides of the synagogue. Instinct drew him to the one with windows dressed in starched lace curtains. He took a deep breath and tapped timidly. The door was opened by a peasant woman, her eyes round with suspicion and astonishment. She turned aside and called nervously to her mistress. A woman appeared, her gentle expression changing into one of fear at the sight of the disheveled, wild-eyed young priest.

"Perhaps you can help me," he said shyly. "I am seeking Rabbi Duvid Malinsky."

"The rabbi? What is it you want with him?" she inquired uneasily.

"Is this his home?" he asked before replying to her question.

"This is his home," the rebbetzin replied, her arms folded across her chest.

He lowered his voice. "My name is Father Peter Kuskov. I am a friend of Yaakov Halevi. I must speak to the rabbi."

The rebbetzin drew back, her mouth agape. Yaakov had often spoken warmly of Father Peter Kuskov. She opened the door and ushered him in briskly.

"Please wait," she said softly. "I will inform the rabbi."

He paced nervously, his eye falling on the beautifully chased silver spice box, *kiddush* cups, and the exquisite, branched candelabra. At the sound of footsteps, he whirled around to face an anxious looking man with a rich, black beard. Peter extended his hand, introduced himself, and muttered an apology.

"I hope you will forgive this unannounced visit, sir," he said tremulously. "I assure you it is most urgent that I see you."

The rabbi brushed the need for apology aside with a smile and wave of his hand.

"Father Kuskov, please refresh yourself," he said, pointing to a screened corner of the room behind which stood a wash basin, soap, and a fresh towel. "Then we will speak."

Minutes later, seated in the rabbi's study, Peter allowed himself the luxury of a glass of strongly brewed tea and some pastries. His hunger eased, he revealed the tragic events of the day.

Rabbi Malinsky listened in stunned silence, his

hands clasped tightly before him. When he finally spoke, his voice was hoarse with pain. "What are we to do?" he said almost to himself.

Father Peter looked at him keenly. "You realize that this goes further than Yaakov himself," he said.

The rabbi nodded. "They are looking for an excuse to start a pogrom, of course."

Father Peter spoke with tight control. "First and foremost, we must find a way to save Yaakov. He will need the best lawyer available, Rabbi. I am certain they are building an ironclad case against the boy. They'll line up their gang of bribed expert witnesses," he said bitterly. "They never have problems finding witnesses ready to spout filthy lies against a Jew, and we…we can only depend on God and His truth, Rabbi Malinsky." His voice filled with emotion, he cried, "We must find a way to save our Yaakov!"

Rabbi Malinsky stared at Peter in open astonishment. "Father Kuskov, Yaakov spoke about you often, about your great love of learning and your growing knowledge of our Talmud. Now I see still another facet of your character that I could never have believed existed in a Russian Orthodox priest. You are a true friend of Yaakov, and, I believe, a friend of *Am Yisroel* as well."

A look of understanding passed between the two men. "Rabbi, we have much to talk about, and in the future, God willing, we will have many opportunities to do so. But for the present, all I can think of is Yaakov. I am terribly afraid for him, terribly afraid," he said with a visible shudder. "You and I know the system. No matter how fine our defense, Yaakov cannot win. There is no justice in our courts, only hatred and violence. The Czar is fearful. There is never enough bread, and the peasants and workers are restless. What better *kaparah*," Father Peter exclaimed, using the Hebrew term, "than the Jews." His voice trembled. "So they are using our little friend, a gentle young man with a heart and soul as pure as the driven snow. They plan to hang him, to provide a circus for the people. And the foul libel will spread on the wings of hatred, and hundreds, maybe thousands, will be martyred. We," he leaned forward, gripping the desk, "we cannot let this happen."

"Father Kuskov, what can be done?" Rabbi Malinsky appealed, spreading his hands before him.

Peter leaned back into the armchair and silently searched for a solution. After a long while, the rabbi excused himself with an apology and left for evening prayers in the synagogue. Upon his return, the two men resumed their discussion over a light supper, which neither ate with much appetite.

"Rabbi Malinsky, there just may be a way," he said, after the rabbi had finished *Birkas HaMazon*.

He drew closer to the rabbi and whispered a plan.

Rabbi Malinsky looked up dubiously. "What you propose is extremely dangerous."

"I know. But is there an alternative?"

The rabbi swallowed hard and shook his head no.

"Then we must begin to map out our strategy," Father Peter pressed.

"Give me a week. There is a lawyer in St. Petersburg who may be in a position to help us. He has important and well-placed friends, and he is known to have handled difficult cases with success. Perhaps I can convince him to represent Yaakov."

Now it was Father Peter who looked doubtful. "Jewish murderers are not popular causes with lawyers."

"I know, but he is still a Jew, and," he sighed, "he knows only too well that he, too, will be a victim if Yaakov is found guilty of murder. I know that we have a long and difficult road ahead of us, Father Kuskov, but when we think of what Yaakov faces, you are right: We have no choice."

Father Peter rubbed his temples. "I know in my heart that Yaakov will remain steadfast in his faith and devotion to his people. But I worry that he will think we have abandoned him. The police are clever. They will try to break his spirit and win a confession from him. If we could only find a way to let him know that he is not alone."

Rabbi Malinsky frowned. "For the present we must depend on Yaakov's faith and intelligence. Hopefully, he will see through their machinations and will decipher their strategy. That is our only hope." He covered his brooding expression with trembling hands. "I admit to still another worry," Rabbi Malinsky murmured. "The story of the murder will spread like wildfire, and I fear for Yaakov's parents. Those poor people have suffered enough, and now this. I must write to them to offer them hope. They must not despair." Then, gazing at Father

Peter's strained face, he leaned toward him and touched his hand. "Neither must we despair, friend."

They shook hands warmly. "We will see each other again soon," Father Peter assured.

Ilya Simonovich Borenstein was a man of imposing stature, with a shock of white hair carefully groomed to voguish length. His aquiline nose rose high and proud in the center of well-defined features; his fashionable goatee was carefully trimmed. There was no doubt that Doctor of Jurisprudence Ilya Simonovich Borenstein was an important man. He wore his success with aplomb, and it oozed from every pore.

Dr. Borenstein's office was located in one of St. Petersburg's most prestigious neighborhoods. No small achievement for a Jew, Rabbi Malinsky mused as he eased into a deep, finely upholstered armchair and gazed at the hundreds of legal volumes that lined the walls. Everyone knew that Ilya Borenstein was welcomed into the rarefied circles of power, his wealth opening the usually tightly sealed gentile doors. Seated across from the fierce looking man, Rabbi Malinsky pondered whether his decision to approach him was wise after all. And if he did accept their offer, could he be trusted to implement their plans?

Dr. Borenstein opened a humidor and offered the rabbi a finely turned cigar, which he politely refused.

"You don't object then if I smoke, Rabbi?" he asked politely. "One of my minor vices," he added with a wicked chuckle.

Rabbi Malinsky smiled hesitantly. The man made him uneasy.

The lawyer chose a cigar with care. He rolled it between his palms, then savored its rich aroma. He snipped the end and lit up, inhaling deeply. Leaning back in his chair, he released a series of smoky circles. "Now dear Rabbi Malinsky, am I to assume that something urgent brings you here?"

Rabbi Malinsky nodded, his heart beating too rapidly. "First let me thank you on behalf of the *kahal* of Volodya for agreeing to see me on such short notice."

Dr. Borenstein waved away the words of gratitude with a flick of his manicured hand. "No need, no need, sir."

"Let me come to the point of this visit, Dr. Borenstein. It is no longer a secret that a young man, a conscript, Yaakov Yitzchak Halevi, the son of the Kronitzer Rebbe, has been arrested and accused of murdering a Christian boy—a baseless accusation, I assure you."

"How can you be certain that this Yaakov Halevi is not indeed a murderer, Rabbi?"

"I know the boy, and not only will I attest to his innocence, but so will the priest serving the community."

Dr. Borenstein's brow arched in disbelief. "A village priest willing to swear the innocence of a Jew accused of murdering a Christian? Well, that is a breath of fresh air. But will he testify in a court of law?"

"He will," Rabbi Malinsky said firmly.

"Hmm. You are certain of his testimony?"

"I am." The rabbi drew in a deep breath. "Dr. Borenstein, will you represent the boy?"

Dr. Borenstein smiled politely. "As a rule, Rabbi, I shy away from controversial cases of this type."

Rabbi Malinsky got up to leave, but the lawyer indicated for him to remain seated.

"But," Dr. Borenstein said, "there is something about this particular case that intrigues me. I have, as a matter of fact, spoken to the investigating magistrate, who hinted broadly, practically told me, that the boy was to be found guilty, no matter what the evidence. The malice of the authorities is so clearly evident that it insults even the pretense of justice."

"That being the case, Dr. Borenstein, what chance does the boy have?"

The lawyer cleared his throat. "If you'll forgive my being blunt, Rabbi, not a chance in a million."

"And if you don't mind my being blunt, Dr. Borenstein, then why accept the case?"

"Rabbi," he replied, a wry smile surfacing, "I may not be the best Jew in the world, but I am a Jew. And this case smacks of evil. I feel that Yaakov Halevi, the son of a noble Chassidic family, deserves his day in court, and I am willing to give those anti-Semites a run for their money."

Rabbi Malinsky sighed deeply. The man before him had a deeper reservoir of character than he had thought.

"Would you agree to come to Volodya to meet a group of men who have taken a special interest in this case, and who will raise the funds for Yaakov's defense?"

"The answer is yes, I would be happy to meet with your committee. But as far as raising funds for his defense, that won't be necessary. Defending an innocent boy will be adequate payment for me," he said sincerely.

Rabbi Malinsky left Dr. Borenstein's office with a lighter heart. On the long ride home, he wondered whether Dr. Borenstein would disassociate himself from them when he learned their true intent. He shut his eyes in prayer. They needed Dr. Borenstein. He must not disavow them. For without the lawyer's support, Yaakov would have no chance at all.

A week later Rabbi Malinsky, Lazar Farbstein, Gershom Lader, and Father Peter Kuskov met with Dr. Borenstein in the rabbi's study. Dr. Borenstein seemed ill at ease in the presence of these determined, intense men.

Father Peter, his face flushed, was anxious to speak. "I must tell you, gentlemen," he began, "about an incident that took place three days ago. I have always had the feeling that the police were playing an ugly and dirty game, and now I know that my feelings were not misplaced."

"Have you uncovered something, Father Kuskov?" Rabbi Malinsky asked.

"I know for certain that the police know the identity of Boris's murderer."

The men gasped.

"But how could you know this?" Dr. Borenstein said incredulously. "What makes you suspect such a thing?"

"Just a few days ago," Father Peter continued, "a village lad came by the rectory. Since he was not one of our regular churchgoers, his visit was, to put it mildly, unexpected. From the moment he came in, I sensed that something was very wrong. The lad was terribly nervous, and he avoided my gaze from the start. I tried to put him at ease, assuring him that whatever he confessed would go no further. It took a great deal of coaxing before he blurted out, `I saw a murder.' He'd been dozing behind a tree, and he'd actually witnessed the fight between Boris and a crony of his, a tough bully named Leonid. In the course of the fracas Leonid picked up a knife lying by the side of the road and stabbed Boris. The boy then went on to tell me that his conscience had goaded him to go to the police. But instead of welcoming the information he reported, he said the police warned him to keep quiet. In fact, he was quite candid about what happened. He said the police threatened him with bodily harm and told him they would put him in prison on a trumped-up charge if he didn't keep quiet. Then to sweeten the threat, they gave him a bribe. Need more be said, gentlemen?"

The men were stunned. "A conspiracy of silence!" Lazar Farbstein moaned. "If we could only get the boy to testify in court, then this nightmare would be over."

Father Peter shook his head. "I only wish it were so simple. But even if I confronted the actual murderer, and he confessed to the police, they would dismiss his confession as the wild rantings of an intimidated peasant boy. They will not let go of their case against Yaakov. When the authorities want a pogrom, no one in this world can stop it."

Gershom turned to Dr. Borenstein, who had been listening quietly to the priest. Now was the time to reveal their plan. But would the lawyer go along, and render the assistance vital to its success?

"You agree that, no matter how superb the defense, there is no chance for Yaakov to be saved?"

The attorney nodded grimly.

"But we think we can give him that chance." And Gershom proceeded to outline the plan they had conceived.

"Will you join us?" Gershom appealed to him.

Before he could reply, Father Peter Kuskov interjected, "You admit that Yaakov is already a condemned man. So what do we have to lose?"

"My reputation, for one," Dr. Borenstein said.

"Is your reputation more valuable than the life of an innocent boy?" Lazar Farbstein fumed.

The lawyer raised his hand in protest. "I did not say such a thing, Mr. Farbstein. But at least you will agree that your proposal won't enhance my reputation?"

The tension in the air lifted, and the men chuckled.

"Although I am uneasy about the plan," Dr. Borenstein continued, "I think it can work, provided that we are very careful. Every step must be meticulously considered, nothing must be left to chance. And the entire plan must remain with us, and us alone. Is that clear?"

"The first order of business will be to have Yaakov transferred to the Fortress of St. Peter and St. Paul in Petersburg," Gershom declared. "And we'll need your help there, Dr. Borenstein."

"That place is a notorious pest hole!" Father Peter cried out.

Dr. Borenstein thought for a moment, then chuckled. "Precisely, my friend. And if only for that reason, they will agree. Naturally, I will point out that a change of venue is necessary for a fair trial, and that a case of such importance should not be tried in a provincial town. That will convince them, I assure you. Our entire plan will hinge on their accepting my suggestion for a change of venue. Is that clear to everyone?"

"Very clear," the rabbi declared. "I think we are on the right road, counselor. Now the hour is late, dear friends. I suggest that we meet next Wednesday evening. We have undertaken a holy task, and a great responsibility rests upon our shoulders. I know that we will not fail. God bless you, all of you, for your good hearts," he said feelingly, embracing each man as he left.

The rabbi then motioned for Father Peter to remain behind. "I would like to discuss another matter with you, Father. Can you spare a few moments?"

Rabbi Malinsky walked over to the hearth and stoked the embers of the dying fire, rekindling its warmth. His back toward the priest, he weighed his next words with care. "Father Kuskov, have you seen Vlad Ruszky since Yaakov's arrest?"

"Curious that you should ask. As a matter of fact, I visited the family last week," he said.

"And how is Vlad taking all of this?" the rabbi inquired.

"Vlad is no fool. He knows that Yaakov is innocent and that this whole business has been fabricated. I wish all of our peasants had as much sense as he does."

Rabbi Malinsky leaned back and closed his eyes, stroking his beard. "I wonder, Father Kuskov, if you would undertake a very delicate mission for me? In fact, I am asking you to perform a great mitzvah."

Father Kuskov stared at the rabbi for a long time, letting the words register. "A mitzvah?" he said eventually. "Rabbi Malinsky, I hope this will be the first of many *mitzvos*."

The rabbi considered his reply for a moment, and he hid a smile. He leaned closer and grasped Father Kuskov's arm.

"First, I must tell you a story." In measured tones and in great detail, he related how Miriam had become Marina.

Father Kuskov sat in silence.

Rabbi Malinsky studied his face. "Now, good friend, I turn to you to right a terrible wrong. Would you speak with Vlad and Katia? You are the only one who can convince them to return Marina, that is, Miriam, to her people and to her rightful heritage." The rabbi paused and took a deep breath. "And no matter how they feel, you must tell Marina the truth. Assure her that she will have a home with my family—more than a home, she will be a daughter to us. I know what I am asking is not easy, particularly for you, Father Kuskov. But you seem to be a unique human being, a man with a great depth of understanding of Judaism and love for the Jewish people.

And it is for this reason that I turn to you. I understand that such a separation will be painful for Vlad and Katia—they love Marina as if she were truly their own. They have not had an easy life, but they are good people, and I have tried to find a small way of compensating them. Assure Vlad that his generosity will be rewarded tenfold. The *kahal* has been negotiating with the widow Kartaly. She is now willing to sell Vlad ten acres of land adjoining the plot he sharecrops for Count Popov. Assure him that all of the papers have already been drawn up."

Father Peter Kuskov's expression was veiled, his face rigid. When he finally spoke, his voice was choked with emotion. "I had no idea, no idea," he said solemnly. "There have been rumors about Marina, but nothing came close to the truth." He shook his head. "This tragic injustice must be righted. And no matter what, I will speak to Marina. She may love her adopted parents but she must know the truth. I pray to God that she will return to her people. The blood of her parents cries out for justice, for her to return to her own people. She will understand this. She must."

Rabbi Malinsky heaved a deep sigh of relief. A faint smile emerged from his beard. He touched the priest's arm. "I could not hope for a better *shaliach*."

Dr. Ilya Simonovich Borenstein entered the Litansky Prison with the brisk step and straight back of one who is at ease in such surroundings. It had taken four months to arrange for a meeting with his client, four agonizingly long months of wondering how the boy was withstanding his solitary confinement.

The lawyer was led into a bleak room and waited impatiently for Yaakov Yitzchak Halevi to enter. He opened his briefcase and ruffled through some papers, all for the sake of the warder, who stood by stiffly and eyed the distinguished man with a mixture of awe and disdain. Dr. Borenstein started as the door clanged open. A tall young man shuffled in, his hands and legs manacled. Despite the chains, the prisoner walked erect, his head held high. Dr. Borenstein was overcome by the young man's dignity.

"I don't believe it is necessary to keep my client in chains while we're together," he said with an ingratiating smile. "Surely you don't think he can escape from here."

"Orders say to keep him shackled," the guard growled.

The lawyer removed two packets of fine tobacco and placed them on the table. "Surely you could perform an act of charity, and one without any risk, wouldn't you agree?"

The warder eyed the expensive tobacco hungrily, then whisked it from the table and shrewdly handed one packet to the guard on duty. He removed the chains and left.

Yankeleh sighed with relief and rubbed his freed wrists and ankles. The lawyer waited a moment before offering an introduction.

"I am Dr. Ilya Simonovich Borenstein," he said in Russian, extending his hand to Yankeleh. "I have been engaged to represent you."

Yankeleh eyed the lawyer suspiciously. Prison life

had taught him to be wary of everyone and everything. He had been exposed to a full bag of their tricks, and he knew only too well that nothing was beneath them.

Once seated and the amenities over, the lawyer lapsed into Yiddish. Yankeleh took in the full measure of this distinguished man and tried to remember where he had heard the name Borenstein. It had a familiar ring. Hadn't Rabbi Malinsky once described a Jewish lawyer with powerful contacts? He searched his memory. Had the man's name been Borenstein?

"First, tell me, Yaakov, how have you been treated?"

Yankeleh smiled ruefully. "I suppose, considering the circumstances, not too badly. They were fearful that their prize prisoner would starve to death before their show trial began, so they even arranged kosher food for me," he said with a cynical grin. "I admit that Mrs. Sokolov's cooking broke my resolve to continue my fast. And recently they even let me out of my cell for some exercise."

"Rabbi Malinsky has been in touch with your parents, Yaakov. They know that we are doing our best for you. Rabbi Malinsky also tells me that you are an intelligent young man, and he believed that you would see through their tactics. It doesn't seem to me that they have broken your spirit," he said with a faint grin. "And I've also learned from the investigating magistrate that you haven't confessed to any of the charges."

"There was nothing to confess to, Dr. Borenstein. I am not a murderer."

The tension eased. Dr. Borenstein seemed to be

what he claimed to be. But still, Yankeleh wondered. He had to be sure.

"How is the rabbi, and…everyone else?"

"All of your friends are fine and stand firmly behind you. Rest assured, no one has been deceived, not the Ruszkys and least of all your very good friend Father Peter Kuskov. Not one of your friends believes the charges against you. Father Kuskov has even unearthed evidence indicating that the police know the true culprit."

"What does that mean? If they know who the murderer is, what am I doing here?"

Dr. Borenstein leaned over and touched Yankeleh's hand. His face was ashen as he spoke: "I am sorry, Yaakov, but the murderer will remain a free man, and you, my dear child, are to be the *kaparah*."

"I…I don't understand."

"Yaakov, by now you must know that in Russia there is no justice for Jews. Right now, the nobles need you as a scapegoat, to keep the people's minds off their empty bellies. Can you see that?"

Yankeleh nodded. "I see only too well, Dr. Borenstein. In that case, why bother with a defense at all? The entire trial will be a sham from beginning to end. Why lend your name to such a mockery?" he said angrily.

"I am here to see justice done, Yaakov. Now, all I ask of you is to listen carefully to what I have to say." He leaned closer. "Yaakov, there will be no trial."

Yankeleh looked incredulous. "What do you mean?"

Dr. Borenstein edged closer, his voice just above a

whisper. "Next Monday you will be transferred to the Fortress of St. Peter and St. Paul in Petersburg. At some point along the way, the police van will be intercepted by men who will appear to be highwaymen. You will probably hear gunfire. Throw yourself to the floor and don't move until someone calls out Kronitz Podolsk. Is that clear?"

Yankeleh swallowed hard. His brow creased in disbelief. He stared long and hard at the grim-faced attorney seated across from him. And then his perplexed expression shifted into a broad grin. "Well, who would have thought?"

At first Yankeleh heard what sounded like the snapping of twigs. He pressed his ear against the van. Gunfire? Raucous voices screaming for help? The two guards exchanged nervous glances. They drew their revolvers, staring malevolently at their manacled prisoner. The shouts and exchange of gunfire grew louder. The guards unbolted the door, peered out, and then leaped to the ground, leaving their valuable prisoner alone.

The sounds grew louder and more threatening. Yankeleh recalled his lawyer's admonition and threw himself to the floor, his hands held protectively over his head. Acrid smoke filled the compartment. Yankeleh coughed and glanced up at the small window, the van's only source of light and air. All he could see was smoke and tongues of flame. He tried to control the fear that gnawed at him as the heat grew in intensity. Smoke curled through the van, and the air was thick with fumes, smothering him. Choking, with what he thought to be his last breath, he cried out, "*Shema Yisroel….*" A voice boomed, "Kronitz Podolsk." Yankeleh tried to turn, but before he could, someone grabbed his legs, and he was dragged from the van seconds before it burst into a ball of fire.

Dazed by the smoke and swiftness of his rescue, Yankeleh took little notice of the masked man carrying him toward the forest. Under cover of twilight and the thick foliage stood a band of masked men. When they saw that Yankeleh was safe and uninjured, they gave a wild victory whoop, mounted their horses and galloped off. The powerfully built man helped Yankeleh to his feet, and, without an exchange of words, made it clear that he was to squeeze into the false bottom of a huge waiting wagon. Before being entombed in its belly, Yankeleh noticed the wagon's contents—an assortment of farm and household equipment.

FIFTEEN

YANKELEH AWOKE SOAKED with perspiration. He sighed deeply, his head resting on the soft pillow. The nightmare of his escape from the jaws of death was a recurrent one. He slipped out of bed, drew on a robe, and made his way quietly to the kitchen, trying not to disturb his wife and children. After splashing cold water on his face, he sat down to sip a glass of tea. He absently fingered the well-worn pages of the *Tehillim* laying on the table, his mind retracing the years.

He thought about the audacity of his rescue and his rescuers. The very boldness of the plan, and the courage and spirit of the men who had carried it out, was almost beyond human imagination. What *chutzpah*, he mused, shaking his head, a smile surfacing through his full, black beard.

Only when they had crossed the border and were well out of range of the Russian border guards had

Gershom Lader allowed Yankeleh to leave his place of hiding. It was then that Yankeleh discovered the identity of his rescuer. During the long journey to Trakai, a city near Vilna, Gershom described how the plan for his rescue had been conceived and executed.

"Why are we going to Trakai instead of Vilna?" Yankeleh asked.

"Our committee feels it is prudent to keep you from the public eye for the time being, or at least until we are certain that the authorities believe you were killed in the attack and your body burned beyond recognition. Meanwhile you will stay with my cousins Yosef and Rivkah Kaganovsky, good, honest people. You'll like them I assure you. And how could they fail but like you, my boy?" he said, thumping Yankeleh on the back good naturedly.

Yankeleh smiled hesitantly. "So the fire was part of the plan?"

"The riskiest part of the plan, that I can tell you. We almost lost you in that blaze," he said with a shudder. "But it was the only way we could be assured that they would not continue to hunt for you."

Yankeleh then voiced his concern for his parents. "If they hear that I was killed," he said, shaking his head sadly, "it will be their end. They will never survive such a blow. They've suffered too much already."

Gershom Lader glanced at Yankeleh, his brow creased. "We'll see what can be done, my boy," he murmured sympathetically.

As they had hoped, the Russian authorities followed

the script to the letter, assuming that highwaymen had attacked and burned their prison van, with the prisoner still inside. If anyone had any doubts, they were afraid to voice them. At the same time, deprived of their show trial, the authorities gave up hope of fomenting a pogrom, and the Jews of the district were safe, for the time being at least. Months later, Yankeleh learned that Gershom Lader had risked his life to travel to Kronitz Podolsk to assure his parents that their son was alive and well. Yankeleh understood only too well the danger of making such a revelation, even to parents. Yet Gershom Lader's humanity and great compassion overcame his better judgment. Yankeleh felt a great debt of gratitude to this unique man. In time, he discovered that many owed their lives to this courageous peddler. To his mind, Gershom Lader was an unsung hero of the Jewish people, a true *tzaddik*.

The years that followed his rescue were exciting ones for Yankeleh, years filled with joy. Yankeleh, the son of the Kronitzer Rebbe, was welcomed wherever he went with honor and affection. The Kaganovskys treated Yankeleh as if he were one of the family, and for the first time in many years Yankeleh was in the bosom of a Jewish home, delighting in its warmth and in the Kaganovskys' seven boisterous and sometimes mischievous children.

When it was deemed safe, he was enrolled in the Vilna Great Yeshiva, where his brilliance shone through like a bright star. The scholarship and quick mind of this scion of a great Chassidic family were soon on the lips of fellow students and rabbis alike. They shook their heads in wonder at Yankeleh, who, though kidnapped from his home at the tender age of thirteen, now was without peer in the yeshiva. For Yankeleh, the very walls of the yeshiva renewed his spirit. He was like a newborn child, eager to explore and to taste everything. His *chavrusah* had difficulty keeping pace with his quick mind, and in time, the *rosh yeshiva* himself, Rav Avraham Moshe ben Shlomo, became Yankeleh's *chavrusah*.

On his twenty-first birthday, *semichah* was conferred on Yankeleh by the *rosh yeshiva*. His parents, though frail of health, travelled to Vilna to be with their son for this auspicious occasion. It was an emotional reunion after a separation of eight years. During their visit the subject of marriage was raised, initiated by a letter received by the Kaganovskys' from Rabbi Duvid Malinsky. The Halevis and Kaganovskys conferred together before they announced to Yankeleh that Rabbi Malinsky had proposed a *shidduch*, a young woman from a good family and with outstanding *middos*. Rivkah Kaganovsky, her eyes sparkling, announced that the girl would be invited to Trakai as soon as possible so the two could meet.

Yankeleh's pulse still quickened when he thought about that first meeting. The Kaganovskys' had gone to great lengths to make their home attractive. A new lace tablecloth adorned the huge, circular table laden with bowls of sumptuous fruit and platters of delicious cakes. Yankeleh entered the room, his eyes averted. He was too fearful and modest to cast his gaze across the room at the girl he knew now sat at the table. When he finally lifted his eyes, he gasped, "Marina! Miriam?"

She smiled and blushed, her own eyes lowered demurely. "I have returned to my people, Yaakov," she said softly, her eyes glistening with tears. There was little more to be said.

On the day of the *tenaim*, Yankeleh handed his *kallah* a leather-bound *Tanach*. "This was given to me by Katia Ivanova a very long time ago," he said, "but it is rightfully yours."

She opened the *sefer* and bit back a cry. Her parents' names leaped out at her, along with her own. For a long moment she remained motionless, staring down at the page. She then handed the *Tanach* back to Yankeleh. "You have cherished this through so many trials. Now, it belongs to both of us. I return it to your care."

Seven years had passed since that day, seven years of contentment. He was now the proud father of five beautiful children, three daughters and two sons. He stroked his beard with satisfaction. He felt fortunate indeed, having known so much joy over the past years, along with one great sadness—the death of his beloved father just the year before.

His father's loyal Chassidim, bereft of their rebbe, had proclaimed Yankeleh the new Kronitzer Rebbe. But a twist of fate anchored him to his Vilna exile. Though the real murderer of Boris Ustyag had been apprehended and he had been exonerated, Yankeleh still was not a free man. As long as the draconian cantonist laws remained in force, he was technically a deserter and would be court-martialed and put to death if he ever entered Russia. With all of his heart he longed to return home, to see the faces of friends and family again, to be at his mother's side now that she was widowed and needed the comfort of a son and the joy of grandchildren. He had pleaded with her to join his family in Vilna, but she stubbornly refused—she would not leave Kronitz Podolsk. Her presence, she explained, would serve as a ray of hope to light the way for the new Kronitzer Rebbe, who would return one day to take upon himself his father's mantle.

The morning broke wet and murky. Yankeleh ignored the rain pelting his face. He was late and was hurrying to the *beis hamidrash* when he was accosted by his student, Yehoshua Herzenberg. The young man seemed in a state of ecstasy—in fact, he clapped his hands for joy.

"Rebbe, have you heard the wonderful news?"

"News?" Yankeleh asked, "What news?"

"Czar Nicholas is dead!" he sang out, his face radiant. "The monster is dead! May his name be blotted out forever."

Yankeleh gasped. "Well, we certainly won't mourn for him," he said, continuing on his way to the synagogue with a brisk step.

When the new czar, Alexander II, assumed the throne in 1855, the Jews of Russia held their breath as one. Filled with trepidation they wondered how they would fare under the new ruler. Would he be as brutal a tyrant as his predecessor? Or would a breath of fresh air sweep away the oppression that Nicholas had left behind as a legacy? Fortunately, Czar Alexander proved to be a more benevolent ruler. Within months, the horrendous cantonist laws were abolished, and at least those Jewish children who had not yet been baptized were returned to their homes.

Yankeleh heard the news from Yehoshua Herzenberg, who burst into his home and blurted out the good tidings. Yankeleh wept, tears of joy streaming down his face.

"My dear wife," he finally said, "God has answered my prayers. At long last, we can go home."

It was one of those rare days in June when the weather is balmy, the sky is a clear azure blue, and the sun is shining with the clarity of fine crystal. Yankeleh gazed out of the carriage window as the morning mist lifted to reveal emerald green meadows blanketed with wildflowers. God's handiwork always left him awestruck, particularly so on this very special day, the day he was returning home.

What Yankeleh did not yet know was that his Chassidim swelled the narrow streets of Kronitz Podolsk eagerly awaiting him, many dancing with delirious joy. In fact, the entire village had taken on a festive atmosphere. The excitement was pervasive. Chassidim from all parts of Russia gathered together, their laughter filling the air as they jostled each other to catch a closer glimpse of their Rebbe.

"I hear the carriage!" one young man called out excitedly.

There was a surge forward as hundreds of men ran to greet the carriage that was bringing their Rebbe home. A loud cheer rose when it came into sight. The carriage drew to a noisy halt and the rebbe stepped out.

"Reb Yankeleh, our Yankeleh!" the crowd called

out, with nary a dry eye among them. Children dashed forward, some grabbing his hand, others his *kapote*. Yankeleh walked into the crowd, trying to sort out the faces from his past. But all he could see was a sea of well-wishers, their laughter mingling with their tears. He turned to the driver of the carriage and instructed him to take his family home. It had been a long and exhausting journey, and they needed to rest. But his own fatigue was forgotten as he gazed into the faces of the hundreds of people milling about him. As he stepped forward, a phalanx of chassidim cut a path for him.

The head of the *kahal*, Baruch Feinsilver, blotted the tears from his eyes and cheeks. "Thank God for this moment," he said. "Yankeleh, that is, Rebbe, I have something that I wish to give you. The moment I heard the wonderful news of your return, I commissioned the writing of a *sefer Torah* in memory of your beloved father."

At that moment, a scribe with an ascetic face framed by a snow white beard emerged from the crowd. He handed Yankeleh a *sefer Torah* cloaked in a royal purple velvet mantle.

"I have never known a greater happiness than having the *zchus* to write this *sefer Torah* in memory of your father, a great man, a noble human being."

Yankeleh held the *sefer Torah* fast, pressed to his heart. He looked into the eager faces of his devoted followers, unable to speak. A *chuppah* was hastily raised above him and Yankeleh strode forward, carrying the *sefer Torah* with its shimmering silver crown and breastplate.

The ecstatic singing and dancing rose to a crescendo. Yankeleh stopped. His brow creased in confusion. Could this be the synagogue of his childhood? The synagogue he remembered was a modest, unadorned, one-story structure. Yet he now stood before a synagogue equal in grandeur to the finest he had known.

"Beautiful, yes?" Feinsilver beamed. "We rebuilt the synagogue in honor of your homecoming," he said excitedly.

Yankeleh glanced at the faces of the *balabatim* waiting to greet him as he brought the *sefer Torah* into its new home. He blinked against the sun streaming in through the tall windows. Some faces were familiar. The *gabbai* and his son stepped forward, their eyes brimming with tears.

"Reb Menachem Mendel," he exclaimed, "and Moshe, my dear old friend, how good it is to see you!"

Moshe bit his lip and sputtered, "Can you find it in your heart to forgive this coward who left you alone in the wilderness?"

"Oy, Moshe, my dear Moshe, you cannot know what joy I felt when I learned that you had been released. Forgive you? What is there to forgive?"

He then looked about him. The synagogue was indeed beautiful. There were rows upon rows of *shtenders* carved of the finest wood, and the *bimah* was of exquisite design. He shook his head in disbelief.

"Come, Rebbe," Moshe urged, after the *sefer Torah* had been placed in the magnificent *aron hakodesh*. "There is someone here I think you will want to see."

He led him through the *shul*, where a youthful chassid was sitting. Reb Yankeleh stared. "Srulik, is it really you?"

The two embraced, their tears mingling.

"I promised myself, my dear friend, that if God, in His infinite mercy, would spare me, I would spread Torah to the four corners of the world. I have become a *maggid*," he said with a smile that revealed the old Srulik. "Who would have believed it, back there in Kirov, that one day you and I would be together again, the Rebbe and his chassid?"

Yankeleh clapped him on his shoulder. "I believed it, Srulik, and my faith has been rewarded."

"Yankeleh, without you…" Srulik's voice caught, "Yankeleh, how many days and nights I thought about you, wanting to thank you for saving my life. And now, now I feel that my words are inadequate."

The Rebbe was drawn forward—so many others to greet, so many good Jewish faces. "Rabbi Malinsky!" he cried out in surprise. "You have come all the way to Kronitz Podolsk for me?" he said, still the young boy standing in awe before his rabbi. Rabbi Malinsky chuckled as he drew him in a warm embrace.

"Yaakov, how could I not be here at this moment? And there is someone else from your past, someone who has come with me to share the joy of your homecoming." Rabbi Malinsky pulled a young man gently by the shoulders.

Yankeleh looked at the handsome chassid with the full, golden beard and eyes as blue as the heavens. He gazed at Rabbi Malinsky with unhidden curiosity. "An old friend?"

"You mean you no longer recognize me, Yaakov?"

The voice had a familiar ring, but the Yiddish was oddly stilted, as if spoken by someone new to the language. He stared up at him. "Peter?" he muttered, his tone reflecting his astonishment.

"You are mistaken, Rebbe. My name is Rabbi Pesach ben Avraham Kuskov," he replied with a twinkle in his eye. "I have come to greet my very first teacher, a young man whose knowledge, courage, and piety led me down the path of truth."

Yankeleh fell on his old friend, hugging him, and finally taking both Rabbi Malinsky and Rabbi Pesach to join him at the head of the table. But before sitting down, he scanned the room again, motioning for Srulik to sit beside him. Yankeleh could not help but hear the murmuring. "Who are these men? These strangers? We have never seen them at the old Rebbe's *tish*." At long last, the Rebbe raised his hand, and a hush fell over the room.

"My beloved chassidim, I am overwhelmed by your welcome and by your generosity and kindness toward both me and the memory of my beloved father of blessed memory. It is not easy for me to stand before you today as your Rebbe, for I know full well that I will never be my father's equal. But with God's help, I will do my best to be worthy of your trust and faith. And now I wish to introduce to you three people who, with God's help, are here with me today: Three men who have walked down a long and painful road with me, sharing my suffering, and offering me hope, inspiration, and comfort."

He turned to Srulik. "Rabbi Yisroel went through the fires of hell with me, and survived as a pious and faithful Jew. Today he stands with me as a friend and as my chassid, and I stand before him in humble admiration."

Yankeleh then turned to face Rabbi Duvid Malinsky and his old friend Peter, now Rabbi Pesach Kuskov. He swept his gaze around the room until the silence was deafening. He clasped his hands together to still their trembling, forcing himself to overcome the tightness in his throat. "I would not be here today if it were not for the courage of Rabbi Duvid Malinsky and Rabbi Pesach Kuskov. They led me from the shadow of the valley of death, with no thought to their own safety. And I feel truly humble before them. I will forever be in their debt, and I will forever be grateful to the *Ribono Shel Olam* for leading me to them and making me worthy of their friendship. Thank you, dear friends, for your devotion and for your noble souls."

Yankeleh swallowed hard. He thought of the people who weren't here with him today, the countless Jewish boys who had been lost to their people, and especially of his first chassid, his old friend Reuven. He wondered with a heavy heart what had become of him.

There was so much more to say, so many feelings to express. He drew himself to full height and gazed out at the sea of admiring faces. His hands extended outward in an all-encompassing embrace, he cried, "It is good to be home."

Printed in Great Britain
by Amazon